ACCLAIM FOR THE WORK OF TRACE CONGER

"Trace Conger is establishing himself as one of the most original voices in crime fiction." - Gregory Petersen, author of *Open Mike* and *The Dream Thief*

"Mirage Man is a propulsive novel that churns with energy and tension." - Vick Mickunas, NPR's Book Nook

"Conger's writing is direct. It moves clearly and quickly, perfect for thrillers." - Ronald Tierney, author of the Deets Shanahan Mysteries

"The Mr. Finn series breathes new life into the P.I. genre… It is one of the best detective series I've ever read." - Gumshoes, Gats and Gams

"*The Prison Guard's Son* is a superbly crafted crime novel. The characters are richly drawn with a rare combination of nuance and depth... This is one of the year's best books." - Mysterious Reviews

"*The Shadow Broker* tips a handsome hat in the direction of old-fashioned pulp fiction and it does so with considerable style. The writing is fluid and the plot pumps along." - Murder, Mayhem & More

THE PRISON GUARD'S SON

A MR. FINN NOVEL

SHAMUS AWARD WINNING AUTHOR

TRACE CONGER

The Prison Guard's Son

This is a work of fiction. Names, characters, places, brands, media, and incidents are either the product of the author's imagination or are used fictitiously. The author acknowledges the trademarked status and trademark owners of various products, brands, bands, and/or restaurants referenced in this work of fiction, which have been used without permission. The publication/use of these trademarks is not authorized, associated with, or sponsored by the trademark owners.

Cover design by 100Covers.

Interior design and formatting by the handsome devils at

Black Mill Books.

ISBN-13: 978-1-957336-14-5

Printed in the United States of America

Library of Congress Cataloging-in-Publication Data

Conger, Trace

For Molly O'Connor.

Dig good ditches.

“No there ain't no rest for the wicked,
until we close our eyes for good.”

— "Ain't No Rest for the Wicked,” Cage the Elephant

“He who fights with monsters should look to it that
he himself does not become a monster.”

— Friedrich Nietzsche

CHAPTER 1

MONSTERS ARE REAL. They hide behind familiar names and faces, and they're capable of entering your safe little world anytime and turning your life upside down. And they can vanish as quickly as they appeared. You may never cross paths with pure evil, but sometimes you do.

Sometimes these monsters walk down your street.

Sometimes they notice you.

And sometimes they follow you home.

SINCE LOSING MY PI LICENSE AND TAKING MY PRACTICE underground three years ago, I had made enough cash and built a solid enough reputation I no longer hustled for work. These days it falls in my lap. That's what happened when Willie Baker called me. He found me the same way all my clients do. Word of mouth. He knew someone who knew someone who put him in touch with me, and here I sat in a city park in Parkersburg, West Virginia, across from the Parkersburg Correctional Facility. It was a fitting location considering Willie was going to ask me to do something illegal, and if I played my cards wrong I might end up in the very building that stood on the other side of the impenetrable razor-wire fence.

Willie had given me enough detail over the phone to entice me to drive the two-hundred miles to Parkersburg, but what he told me in the next fifteen minutes would determine whether I took his case or not.

I arrived twenty minutes early and grabbed a seat at a park bench under a giant oak tree. It was mid November and many of the trees had already dropped their leaves. Those trees that hadn't yet surrendered to fall painted a backdrop of orange, yellow and red hues. A group of children collected a pile of downed leaves and plowed through them, their arms spread wide and their heads tilted back, mouths open laughing. They looked like airplanes flying through vibrant-colored clouds. Their mothers looked on and smiled, probably wanting to join in.

A moment later loose gravel popped under a vehicle's tires. It was a Ford Econoline van with a prison logo on the door. It belonged to the large gray building across the street, the one with the shitty views and the bars on the doors. The van parked next to my Lincoln Navigator and an older man stepped out of the vehicle. He closed the door and without locking it limped across the parking lot toward me. A gray Walmart shopping bag dangled from his right hand. The bag sagged under the weight of the papers inside, some of which had pierced the thin lining in an attempt to escape, and I thought the bottom might fall out before he made it to the bench.

"Mr. Finn?" he said.

I slid to my left. "Have a seat."

He shook my hand and sat down. "It's nice to meet you. Thanks for helping me."

"I haven't agreed to help you yet, Mr. Baker. But I am anxious to learn more about your situation."

From our call, I knew the man sitting next to me in the unwashed blue prison guard uniform and Carhartt work jacket wanted me to find the two men who murdered his son, Josh, in 1984. He explained how the two men responsible were arrested, tried and convicted, and how they were released in 1992 after serving only eight years in some detention center for fuckups.

Willie Baker, much like the rest of Parkersburg, felt eight years was a bit light for what they did to his son, and now he wanted to levy his own justice. I didn't discuss details over the phone, which is why we sat next to each other feeling the November breeze whip across the playground.

"Start from the beginning," I said. "Just so I know I didn't misunderstand you on our first call."

Baker grabbed his left pants leg with his right hand and pulled it up so his left leg crossed the other. He leaned back against the hard park bench and drew in a deep breath.

"It was in eighty-four. My wife had taken Josh to the mall to do some Christmas shopping. They were in a store when my wife turned around and Josh was gone." He crinkled the bag between his fingers. "My wife was always so careful with him, and she only turned her back for a minute. But that's all it took. He was gone. Mitz and the saleswoman tore the store upside down, but they didn't find him. He had wandered out into the mall and disappeared."

"How old was your son when all this happened?"

"He was four." Baker paused. "He would have been thirty-seven next month."

"Go on," I said.

"It was a weekend and I was home working on our car. It was the only car we had and Mitz had to borrow my brother's Impala to go to the mall. She was gone for a few hours. Then she comes home and jumps that Impala over the curb and almost hits the tree in our front yard. She runs into the garage yelling about how they took Josh. I get her to calm down enough so that she can tell me what happened. She's crying and she yells 'they can't find him.' I'm listening to her but I'm not putting it all together. Then I notice Josh isn't in the car and it hits me. She tells me he wandered off. Said she went to the mall security office. They asked around, made an announcement over the PA, talked to the clerks to see if anyone remembered seeing him, but there was nothing. He was gone. One minute he's there and the next, he's not. Gone into thin air."

"So she went to the police?"

"The mall called the police. Mitz called me several times but I was under the car in the garage and didn't hear the phone ring."

"What did the police do?" I said.

"They interviewed my wife and me. She told them the same story I just told you. That night they put Josh's picture on the TV. On the local news. Then they called us at home the next day to tell us they found him." He dropped his head and grabbed the bag with his hands so tight I thought he might rip it in two. "They found his body next to an abandoned tobacco shack a few miles from our house."

"The two boys you mentioned on the phone. Tell me about them."

"Jacob Vance and Raymond Turner. I'll never forget 'em. Both nine years old at the time. Local boys. They took him from the mall."

"Did they know your son? Or your family?"

"No. Never seen or heard of them before. The police figured Josh just walked away from Mitz and into the mall and these two boys found him walking by hisself and lured him away."

"No motive?"

"Except for being sick in the head, no."

"How did the police find them? The boys?"

"A woman saw the TV news the night they showed Josh's picture. She remembered seeing a neighbor boy from down the road earlier in the day walking with a boy who looked like Josh. She called the police. The cops interviewed him and his buddy--Vance and Turner--and one of them confessed to everything. Confessed about how they took him from the mall and into the woods. And..." He wiped his eyes. "And how..."

"That's enough," I said, not wanting him to relive the hell he probably experienced every day since eighty-four. "I don't need to know anything more about your son, but tell me about the boys. What is it you want me to do?"

"I want them boys dead. I want someone to take a hammer and crush their skulls just like they did to my little boy."

"I find people, Willie. I don't kill them."

"I know. I only want you to find them. I've already made arrangements for someone else to kill 'em. All I want you to do is tell me where there are."

"Seems like a long time to be waiting for revenge," I said. "Why now? If they've been out for so long, why go after them now?"

"After Josh was killed, Mitz and I had to get through everything together. We were all that we had. I knew if I did something stupid the police would take me away, and I wasn’t sure Mitz was strong enough to make it on her own. But she died of ovarian cancer last year. With Mitz gone, I've got no reason to hold back anymore. I'd do it myself if I were younger. And if I could find them."

"If something happens to these two, you're the first person the police will come for."

"I know, but I work at the prison six days a week. I'll have an alibi." He smacked his leg with his right hand. "And with this bum leg, no one'll believe I'd be able to catch and kill two men." He looked at the prison and then back at me. "I've got two-hundred-thousand dollars saved up. Most of that was Mitz's life insurance. I don't know if it's enough, but it's all I got. I want you to tell me where they are. Both of them. I'll take care of the rest."

"No offense Willie, but this job seems too easy. You could find any number of PIs who could locate these two for a fraction of what you're offering me. Why not save your money and go with someone else?"

"These two aren't going to be easy to find. Trust me, I've hired it out before. Just the locating part. I never told anyone about what I wanted done to them. Went through a few other PIs. They turned up nothing."

"So why me?"

"After Vance and Turner were released in 1992, the state didn't think they would be safe. That what they did to my boy was so heinous their lives would be in danger. Can you believe that, *their* lives? Never mind what they did to my family. The government gave them new identities and shipped them off to God knows where. And that's it. New names and new locations. And I'm stuck back here to mourn my boy who never got the chance to grow up. None of the people I hired came close to finding them because Jacob Vance and Raymond Turner don't exist anymore. What I need is someone who can find their new identities." He looked over his shoulder and spoke low. "So I can give my boy the justice he deserves."

I'd never heard of the government using witness protection to safeguard anyone except federal witnesses. Not our government anyway. "That adds quite the dynamic, Willie."

"I know it does. That's why I need someone who can do it right. Those two have to pay the real price for what they did to Josh." He handed me the plastic bag. "That's the police file. It's everything I got. Don't make your decision without reading it. Look at it and see what those two boys did to my son, and if you want to pass then that's fine. I'll look for someone else to help me."

I took the bag and set it on my knee to keep it from breaking open. The tall tower of the Parkersburg Correctional Facility stared down at me, as if daring me to take the case.

"I'll review your information, Willie, but you have to be prepared for me to say no. If these guys really are in WITSEC then they'll be difficult as shit to find."

"Difficult but not impossible," said Willie. He stood up. "All I ask is that you consider it. I have to get back to work."

"I'll let you know as soon as I can," I said.

Willie limped across the park moving faster than when he arrived. Maybe he was late for his shift, or maybe he felt lighter having handed off the information on his long dead son, like some burden lifted. Or maybe he moved faster because he was thinking about the two responsible for his son's death getting what he thought they deserved.

After Willie pulled out of the parking lot I turned to see the group of children still plowing through the hand-raked mounds of leaves a few hundred feet away. Their mothers still looked on with a hint of jealousy. Part of me wanted to stay and watch, but the other part urged me off the bench and into my car. I had some reading to do.

CHAPTER 2

THE PLASTIC BAG Willie gave me contained photocopies from his son's case file. It included police reports, coroner report, transcribed court testimony, Vance's and Turner's 1984 booking photos, handwritten interview notes and a few other documents. Together they painted a gruesome image of what happened that November afternoon thirty-two years ago.

According to the information, after they left the mall Vance and Turner made Josh walk two miles through an upscale neighborhood, a city park and a wooded area until they reached the tobacco shack. Images from multiple mall security cameras captured Vance and Turner leaving the mall, Josh between them, each holding one of Josh's hands. Timestamps on sequential photos indicated only two minutes passed from the time Josh first encountered Vance and Turner until the time all three walked out the mall's front entrance. Two minutes to snatch a kid and vanish in broad daylight.

Medical reports showed Josh had been sexually assaulted, tortured and had suffered repeated blows to the head and body, presumably with rocks. His body revealed multiple fractures to the skull, a broken arm, cuts to the cheek and lips and several marks on his back that resembled the heel of a thick-soled boot. The pathologist also found traces of modeling glue in Josh's eyes and theorized that Vance and Turner tried to glue his eyes shut. The official cause of death was blunt force trauma to the head.

Several witnesses testified they had seen the two boys with Josh. One man said they walked past him in the park, but he didn't think anything suspicious until he saw Josh on the news that evening. Another woman saw the three boys on her street and recognized Raymond Turner, who lived on her block. After seeing the news segment she directed the police to Turner's house.

A white envelope, softened with age, contained a series of photographs revealing what investigators discovered when they arrived at the tobacco shack. The photos captured various angles of Josh lying chest down, his right cheek seemingly floating in a pool of blood. A crimson trail leading somewhere beyond the edges of the photos indicated he had been dragged from one spot to another. A few of the photos showed Josh's body covered with jagged wooden boards, probably pulled from the dilapidated tobacco shack, in a crude attempt to conceal the body.

Feeling my stomach tightening, I turned my attention to the police booking photos of Jacob Vance and Raymond Turner. The photos showed the two standing in front of a height chart. Vance stood four-feet-eight-inches tall and Turner was two inches shorter. They each held a small whiteboard with their name, social security number, booking date and some type of case number written in thick black marker.

Both boys had short hair, but while Vance had a buzz cut, Turner had more of a tousled style that reached his eyebrows and covered part of his ears. From what I could see in the booking photos, Turner's hair looked similar to Josh's. Neither looked like a cold-blooded killer, but what nine-year-old did?

I slipped the photos back into the envelope and swapped it for the police report. According to the report, when the police asked Raymond Turner about Josh, he immediately confessed to his role in the abduction. Then he rolled on Vance and the police picked him up within the hour.

During questioning they both admitted to kidnapping Josh and leaving him near the tobacco shack, but they said he was alive when they left. When it came to the actual assault, each said it was the other who beat, sexually assaulted and killed the boy.

Vance and Turner later recanted their admissions, but evidence, including footprints at the crime scene that matched the boys' boots, forensic tests confirming modeling glue residue on Turner's T-shirt and blood spatter on Vance's clothes, which the police found in a garbage can outside his home, was all the proof the court needed.

Even though Vance and Turner were only nine years old, they were tried as adults. The court found both guilty of murdering Josh Baker and remanded them to the ironically named Pleasant Hill juvenile detention facility forty miles outside of Parkersburg for at least eight years. Even though they went to big-boy court, they were too young to go to prison. According to a few newspaper clippings, the court sealed the trial records, which made me wonder how Willie had compiled the information that now littered the inside of my Navigator.

I thumbed through the heaps of paper until I came across a pale yellow sticky note with an address for Evergreen Cemetery. I keyed the address into my GPS and fifteen minutes later I rolled through the iron gates at 2601 14th Avenue. The attendant on duty showed me where to find Josh Baker's gravesite.

After a brief walk past chipped headstones and grass that seemed too tall I found Josh's two-foot-tall grave marker. Two carved angels flanked an image of Josh's face etched on the front. As I stood there, I thought of my own eight-year-old daughter, Becca. With the exception of my divorce from her mother, Becca's life had little disruption. Her two overprotective parents rarely let her want for anything, something we'd probably regret in her teenage years. Becca lived in a safe and loving environment. She spent her days playing with dolls, making crafts, reading books and laughing with friends. Violence never reared its ugly face around her. For Becca, life was only sunshine and rainbows. I imagined Josh Baker's life was much the same until the day he met Jacob Vance and Raymond Turner. What did he do that morning? Was he excited to see the Christmas decorations at the mall? What did Vance and Turner tell him to convince him to follow them? How many times did he ask for his mother? Did he ever try to turn back as they led him further away from safety?

Beneath the etching of Josh's face was an inscription. I ran my fingers across the cold smooth surface, tracing the letters.

JOSHUA STEPHEN BAKER
BELOVED SON
WE LOVED YOU WITH ALL OUR HEART
BUT GOD NEEDED YOU MORE IN HEAVEN
THAN HE NEEDED YOU ON EARTH

Bullshit, kid. God didn't take you. Two sick fucks did.

I jerked my phone out of my inside coat pocket, searched through the call history and dialed.

"Hello?" said the familiar voice on the other end.

"I'll take your case, Willie. I'll let you know what I find, but sit tight. It might take some time."

I hung up the phone before he could respond.

CHAPTER 3

THE DRIVE back to Cincinnati gave me three-and-a-half hours to think about the quagmire I'd stepped in. This would be a tough case and I was already emotionally invested, which made me nervous. I always separated my work from my emotions because what I do requires a clear head. Emotions screw things up. It's like landing an airplane. You don't want your pilot thinking about some melodramatic bullshit when he should be focused on landing a one-hundred-ton aircraft careening toward a narrow asphalt runway at 120-miles-per-hour.

Josh Baker got a raw deal at the hands of two sociopaths and all I could think about was finding Vance and Turner, tying them to my rear bumper and dragging them back to West Virginia. In the pothole lane.

But something else bothered me, something I had dismissed until now. Vance and Turner killed Josh Baker thirty-two years ago. That's a lot of time to figure your shit out and change your ways, but was that possible for two kids? Not even fully formed, mentally or physically, nine year olds who kidnapped and beat the life out of a four-year-old boy a month before Christmas? West Virginia didn't give Willie an executioner, so he planned to hire his own after I unearthed Vance's and Turner's whereabouts. That made me responsible for their deaths. While I didn't have a problem with the idea as I stood over Josh's grave, after reflecting on it I knew the decision wasn't that easy. Consequence is a nasty bitch. Vance and Turner would meet her at some point, but if they'd turned their lives around, could I still give Willie's triggerman what he needed to put them down?

I kicked the doubt out of my head. No need wasting time on the emotional blowback until I had something to worry about. There were three-hundred-and-twenty million people in the United States and finding two of them, two people who didn't exist anymore, would be as easy as Chinese algebra after a bottle of tequila. And all I had to work with was a battered bag of files that had yellowed with age and a single photograph each of what Vance and Turner looked like before the puberty stick smacked them in the face.

Four scenarios loomed over me. One, Vance and Turner could be dead. And while that made the up-or-down vote on whether they lived a moot point, it didn't make finding them any easier. If locating a living person with a government identity was hard, finding a dead person with a government identity was damn near impossible. My only hope would be for an obituary to tie them to their West Virginia roots, but that was a moonshot.

Two, the government could have relocated them outside the country. I knew my way around the information channels in the States, but those channels got murkier the farther you traveled across the border. If they were in Canada or Mexico, I could probably still find them, but if they moved to Belgium, forget about it.

Three, Vance and Turner could have returned to prison. I'm not a criminologist and I couldn't psychoanalyze my way out of Willie's Walmart bag, but I had a hard time thinking these two were capable of leading normal lives after what they did. About seventy percent of violent offenders step in shit again, so the likelihood was high that at least one of these two asshats was behind bars or had done a stretch sometime between being released in 1992 and now. Finding an inmate only takes a call to the Federal Bureau of Prisons, but if Vance and Turner landed back in the system they would be there under their new names and anyone answering the prison hotline would not know about their past.

Scenario four was the most likely. Uncle Sam relocated them to parts unknown, USA. Of the four scenarios, this offered the best chance for finding them. If they were still in the country, they were within reach. I assumed WITSEC provided the average relocation package to some small town in the Midwest, not an expensive international destination, so I decided to focus my effort on native soil.

Locating people is equal parts art and science. A good investigator can find most people with a laptop, an Internet connection and a free afternoon. I don't deal with the "most people" slice of the population. I deal with the people who are actively evading someone. The ones who disappear and don't want to be found. Searching for two people with no names or known locations didn't unnerve me, since those are the usual suspects on my to-do list. But the process gets complicated when government identities are involved.

Vance and Turner were invisible and that required a different approach. Scientists don't find black holes by looking at them. They find them by looking at the ripples around them. That's how I'd find Vance and Turner. By looking at the ripples. And that meant starting with their families and friends. If I was lucky I would stumble upon a breadcrumb and that would lead me to the sandwich, and then the motherfucker holding the mayo.

WHEN I ARRIVED HOME THAT AFTERNOON I FOUND MY FATHER, Albert, and my ex-wife, Brooke, sitting on the sofa watching *Columbo*.

"How was coal country, son?" asked Albert. "You get black lung?"

"Don't think so. Just a bad case of cramped knees from the drive." I wondered why my ex-wife was there. "You two throwing me a surprise party or something?"

Brooke stood up and hugged me as Albert squinted at the television. "What took you to West Virginia?" she said, running her hand across the beard I had refused to shave for the past two months.

"House call. What brings you here?"

"I can't just stop by?" she said.

"I'm not saying you have to file a form or anything. Just not used to seeing you pop up unless you're dropping Becca off."

"I had the day off and Becca is at a friend's house. I got bored so I thought I'd come by and see what you two were up to."

"Well, it looks like Albert's halfway through the *Columbo* box set he found at the library."

"It's a good show," he said.

"It's a terrible show," I said. "It's entirely formulaic. Look for the guest star and that's your murderer."

Albert rolled his eyes. "*Columbo* isn't about figuring out who did it, it's about how he's going to catch 'em." He pointed a thumb at Brooke. "Your wife likes it."

"Ex-wife" we said in unison.

"That doesn't mean much." I smiled. "She always had shitty taste in television."

"And men." Albert laughed.

"It's not bad," said Brooke. "I've been watching it for three hours. You'd think he'd get a better car. That one looks like it could fall apart at any minute."

"The car is part of the mystique," said Albert.

I moved to the kitchen to escape the conversation, hoping Brooke would follow. She did.

"So what was in West Virginia?"

"I met with a client about a missing person case."

"You going to be spending a lot of time there? In West Virginia?"

"Looks like it, for starters anyway. This case... I think it's going to keep me moving. I don't have a lot to go on, just decades-old police reports, but I could be out of town for a while."

"What about Becca?" asked Brooke.

When Brooke and I split up five years ago we decided to share custody of our daughter. She stayed with me on the weekends and lived with Brooke the rest of the week. Becca was the most important thing in my life and I didn't make a habit of missing our time together. I had only missed one weekend together since the divorce, but I knew I was going to have to postpone the next few sleepovers. I wasn't sure where this case would take me and I couldn't jet home every weekend.

"I'm not sure how long I'll be on the road, but I'm sure Albert can pinch hit while I'm out. Maybe introduce her to *Columbo*."

Brooke looked disappointed.

"I'm sorry. I don't want to miss out on any time with her and I plan to make it up to her when I'm back."

Brooke brushed a finger across the back of my hand and lowered her voice. "Maybe we can all spend more time together when you get back."

"What about Dr. Dickhead?" Since our split Brooke had been shacking up with Dr. Daryl Jennings, an anesthesiologist at the hospital where she worked. He ran into trouble a year ago when he fell into a fentanyl smuggling ring. While I got him out of trouble with the Indianapolis mob, there wasn't much I could do to get him out of trouble with Brooke. I knew that things between them had been rocky since then, but I just assumed they'd work it out because they always did.

"We're no longer seeing each other," she said. "He's agreed to stay at a hotel until Becca and I can find a place of our own."

"You broke up with him and kicked him out of his own house? That's pretty cold."

"I figured you'd be happy about it."

"I was never his biggest fan, given that, you know, you moved in with him the day after we split. Kind of makes a guy wonder."

"I'll be the first to admit it was a mistake. A stupid one. Hindsight, right? He was a security blanket. For me and for Becca. A way out of whatever you and I had once it started to crumble." She brushed a long strand of red hair from her face. "And I'm sorry. I hope I can make it up to you. And right now I don't even know what that means."

My living room, with *Columbo* blaring in the background, wasn't the ideal place to dwell on the shitty parts of our relationship, so I changed the subject.

"Maybe you can solicit Albert's real estate services and he can help you find a new place." I fanned my open hand across the room like a *Price Is Right* model showing a deluxe dining room set. "He did find us this lavish abode."

She laughed. "I should go. If I stay any longer I'm going to get sucked into more television with your father." She checked her watch. "I need to pick up Becca anyway. Let me know when you finish your case and consider what I said. You know, about spending some time together."

"I'll give it a noodle." I walked her to the door. After she yelled a goodbye to Albert, who stayed glued to the television screen, she put her hand on my waist and kissed me longer than she had in years.

"Good luck on whatever you're working on." She started out the door, but stopped and turned. "And Finn. I like the beard."

"Thanks," I said, watching her walk down the breezeway.

CHAPTER 4

AFTER BROOKE LEFT I strolled past Albert, still transfixed by Lieutenant Columbo's detective skills, and slipped into my office.

You can't trust many people in this business. Willie Baker had an agenda—he wanted Vance and Turner dead. And while I had no reason to doubt his story about their government protection, something didn't sit right about the Feds protecting two child killers. The whole idea seemed ridiculous, but it wasn't the first time I'd used that adjective to describe the government.

It's possible what Willie told me was the real deal, but I'd been fooled before. That's why I wanted to get as much information as I could on Jacob Vance and Raymond Turner before diving too deep into this case.

I scrutinized the bag Willie had given me. It's easy to fabricate a case file, especially since the real case file would be sealed and even I would have a hard time getting that. Right now the only background information available was a stack of photocopies and I had no idea if they were legitimate or not.

The first thing I wanted to know was if Josh Baker really was beaten to death and left next to a tobacco shack in Parkersburg. That wouldn't be hard to confirm because the press would jump all over something that horrific, especially in small town, West Virginia. A quick LexisNexis search revealed a string of articles from the *Charleston Daily Mail* and the *Parkersburg Sentinel* that corroborated the details Willie shared. The clips didn't identify the two boys because they were minors at the time and were protected from being outed publicly. A reporter named Nell Richards filed a dozen bylines during the trial. I jotted her name in my notepad and moved on.

I also wanted to verify if Vance and Turner had entered WITSEC and dropped off the face of the earth. Had they gone under, all traces of their existence would be swept under the rug. Maybe Willie got his facts wrong and these two just left town after being released from the juvenile detention center. Or maybe the WITSEC story was just a rumor started to cover their tracks and deter anyone from looking for them. Willie said he had hired other PIs to find them and they all came up short. If that was true, then I suspected Vance and Turner really were in WITSEC. Otherwise, someone else would have already found them.

Social security numbers are the gold standard for PIs trying to locate someone. That's because most personal records are searchable using a social security number, including marriage and divorce records, banking information, residence histories, bankruptcies, judgments, employment histories, criminal records… you name it. If those numbers were still active, which they shouldn't be if Vance and Turner went into protection, I could generate a report with all the information required to find them. If those numbers were inactive, it meant they really did go under.

I grabbed their social security numbers from the booking photos and ran a trace. I hoped to get an employment hit confirming that one of them was collecting a paycheck from a Best Buy somewhere in Minneapolis, but that didn't happen. All activity linked to their social security numbers ceased in 1992, the year they left detention.

That told me the government scrubbed their original numbers and assigned new ones.

New numbers get assigned all the time. If someone is a victim of identity theft and their credit turns to shit, they can apply for a new social security number and hit reset. When the government assigns new numbers they keep the old numbers in the system. It's like retiring a baseball player's jersey, but instead of hanging on the side of a grand stadium it collects dust in a government database. And since Vance's and Turner's numbers hadn't been touched since 1992, they had a lot of dust on them.

Vance and Turner were off the grid, and the theory the Feds reassigned them new identities fit. The story Willie told me held up and I was ready to move on to the next step and research the hell out of everyone involved.

CHAPTER 5

I WORK ALONE. Most of the time. I don't like people knowing the details of my cases for obvious reasons, but I can't do everything myself. Some information and certain skills are beyond my reach. That's why I rely on a few trusted individuals for support from time to time. Cricket is one of the professionals in my tool bag.

Cricket is a jack-of-all-trades, and most of those trades are illicit. I don't know where he gets his information, but he's damn good at getting it. He's also a whiz at farming out special projects for people like me. Need to hack a cell phone photo bank? He can get it done. Need someone to park outside your home and sit watch with a Street Sweeper in his lap while you sleep safe and sound inside? He'll do it. Need to reconstruct a fifty-year-old birth certificate with a raised seal from South Dakota? He's your man.

Truth is, there hasn't been much I've thrown Cricket's way that he was unable to handle with speed and discretion. Unfortunately he doesn't come cheap, and since our skill sets overlap in certain areas I only turn to him for the stuff I can't do myself.

On a personal level I didn't know much about Cricket. Other than his first name is Jim, which somehow led to the nickname "Jiminy Cricket" or Cricket for short. He's tall and boney with sunken cheeks, and the kind of thin that makes him look like he's sick and undergoing some medical treatment, though as far as I know he's as healthy as me. I hadn't used him in a year, but I needed his help on this one.

I dialed his number and he answered on the second ring.

"Cricket, I need a favor."

"What's that?"

"You have access to any age progression software?"

"I know someone who dabbles in it."

"Is it accurate?"

"Depends on the source photo. If you've got a good photo, the software can generate a pretty accurate image. Of course, criminals have been known to change their appearance, Finn."

"Does it work with kids?"

Cricket drew in a deep breath and sounded annoyed at my questions. "You mean like one of those missing kids they put on milk cartons? The then and now shots?"

"Something like that."

"It's going to work better on adults since we don't change that much over time, but it can do kids too. You're probably looking at less accuracy though. I'd guess kids' facial features tend to change over a decade or more. Adults don't."

I pulled Vance's and Turner's booking photographs from the case file and ran a finger across the smooth images. "If I get you photos of two kids, can you tell me what they might look like now? Assuming they haven't done anything drastic to alter their appearance?"

"You working with missing kids now, Finn? Trying to get into heaven?"

"No," I said. "That ship sailed. Caught fire. And sunk."

He laughed. "How old would they be now? The older you go the less accurate it'll be."

"They're nine years old in the photo and they'd be forty-one now."

"Why you looking for two forty-one-year-old missing persons? Don't you think they'd be old enough to find their way back home by now?"

"I told you, they're not missing."

Cricket didn't say anything.

"So," I said, "will it work or not?"

"That's a big leap, but it's your money if you want to try it. Whenever I've seen that technology it's to identify someone over a five or six-year span at the most. Not..." He did the math in his head. "That's thirty-two years."

"I know. Can you do it?"

"It might take a few days," said Cricket. "My guy is in Vegas and no telling how busy he is. Send me the photos along with the dates they were taken and I'll see what he can do." He paused. "While you're at it send me your photo and I'll show you what you'll look like in twenty-three years."

"No thanks. I'd rather not know."

CHAPTER 6

I WOKE up the next morning thinking about why the government would relocate and assign new identities to two child killers. The WITSEC program protects criminals and others who have testified in federal cases, but Vance and Turner didn't testify against anyone. Instead, they kidnapped and crushed a little boy's skull with rocks and their boot heels. It didn't seem fair to protect them from the shitstorm they'd whipped up. I get that they were only nine and had no chance at a normal life, but it was still a hard pill to swallow. Having a daughter myself, I understood why Willie wanted to find and bury these two shitstains.

The WITSEC program is a coordinated effort between the DOJ and the US Marshals service. The DOJ authorizes the program and decides when to use it and the Marshals Service protects those individuals unlucky enough to have to participate. I didn't know much about the inner workings of the program, aside from what I'd seen in movies or read about in Elmore Leonard novels, but I knew someone who did.

Aside from Cricket, another person I relied on from time to time was Gypsy Scott.

Gypsy Scott was in some ways my direct opposite. While I

made a living finding people who didn't want to be found, he made his living by helping people vanish into thin air. New name, new location, new job, new background, new everything. He essentially does what WITSEC does, but he offers his services to anyone willing to pay a seven-figure fee. No federal testimony required. He's consulted with WITSEC more than once to help the government relocate high-value assets and he knows his shit. I hadn't seen Gypsy Scott in two years, but it was time to remedy that.

Gypsy Scott ran his operation from a Victorian house in Newport, Kentucky. His home belonged on a brochure for a New England bed and breakfast. It's taupe with maroon and cream accents and trim, and the two-story turret has more angles than a protractor factory.

I parked on the street, walked up the winding paver stones that led to the wide, covered front porch and knocked on the door. A moment later a short woman in her seventies with a gray wig too large for her head cracked the maroon door.

"Well, well. Look what the cat dragged in, kicked and spit on," she said, eyeing me over her glasses. "He expecting you?"

I wiped my feet on the doormat, across the image of a .357 magnum. "No," I said. "But I'm hoping to get a few minutes with him. He in?"

She glanced over her shoulder. "He better be." She opened the door wide. "Come on in then, you're letting all the heat out." As I walked past her I noticed the revolver in her right hand. She directed me to the waiting room with a flourish of her unarmed hand. Thick plastic bracelets jangled on her thin arms while a diamond ring the size of a Maine Coon cat sparkled on her bony finger.

As I sat down on a thick padded chair with paisley print she slid open the double doors to Gypsy Scott's office, ducked her head in and said something in a language I couldn't understand. Polish maybe. Then she sat down behind the large oak desk in the waiting area and stared at me.

"Still doing your PI thing?"

"Yep."

"How's that going?"

"Good."

"You here for a client or yourself?"

"Just wanted to get some information for a case." I gestured toward the doors she had just closed. "Figured he could give me some insight."

She nodded her head and looked at me over her glasses again. "You in trouble?"

"Not that I'm aware of." I looked at my watch. "But it's still early."

"Uh huh," she said.

Gypsy Scott and I met eight years ago. He was working a pro bono case helping a woman and her son disappear from her gang-banger husband. The husband ran drugs and guns into California, and he beat the shit out of her and her five-year-old son one too many times. I helped Gypsy Scott locate the family at a gang safe house and he worked his magic behind the scenes to establish new identities for the woman and boy. While her husband was out of town, we slipped in, snatched the pair and relocated them to Boulder, Colorado. Papa never knew what happened to them, but they were safe and out of his reach forever.

The pocket doors slid open. Gypsy Scott stood in the doorway. He wore torn jeans, a white T-shirt underneath a black zip-up hoodie and blue-and-white boat shoes.

"Well shit me Skittles," he said. "Come on in!"

I nodded to the woman and followed him into his office. Two long white drawstrings bounced across his shoulders as he walked.

"It's been awhile," he said, shutting the doors. "What brings you across the river?"

"I need some information."

"First minute is free, then I have to charge you." He smiled and poured me a cup of black coffee from a pot he kept on his desk.

"You ever hear of Jacob Vance or Raymond Turner?"

He cocked his eyebrows and shook his head. "No. Should I have?"

"Back in eighty-four, when they were nine years old, Vance and Turner killed a little boy in West Virginia. Pretty gruesome stuff. According to the records they did time in some kiddie camp and when they were released they were assigned new identifies and shuffled off somewhere never to be heard from again."

He rubbed his chin and sat on the edge of his desk. "No, never heard of it. So they were assigned new identities for their own protection? Because Uncle Sam thought someone would come looking for them once they got out?"

"Right."

He shook his head again. "I've heard of a few high-profile cases in the UK and Canada where that happened. Killer kids. But never heard of anything like it in the States. You sure you got your facts right?"

I nodded. "I read the case file."

"Surely the case file didn't mention anything about new identities? It wouldn't be in there."

"No, that came from the victim's father. He had a theory the Feds wrapped them in new names and shipped them off somewhere. I looked into them and the paper trail ends in ninety-two. It checks out. But nothing about it in the local paper."

"There wouldn't be," he said. "If the Feds were involved, they would've issued a gag order on the press. You won't find anything official. It's not like today where you've got citizen journalists running a hundred different blogs and discussing all this shit online. Information was much easier to control and suppress back then." He looked up at me. "So how are you involved in all this?"

"The victim's father hired me to find these two."

"And do what with them? Assuming you find them."

"That's patient-doctor info." I fought back a smile.

"Right. So how can I help? Understanding I've never heard of these two kids."

"You know more about WITSEC than anyone I know. I wanted to see if you've got any ideas on where to begin."

"That's assuming they're actually part of WITSEC. Officially, that program is reserved for high-value assets testifying in federal cases. Mob stuff. But still, if these two guys are being protected, I'd assume the government would do it through the WITSEC program even though they aren't federal witnesses. I mean the infrastructure is already there, so it makes sense the DOJ would run it."

"I figured."

Gypsy Scott slid his wire-rim glasses down the bridge of his nose and stared at me. "I don't think I can do much to point you in the right direction, other than to tell you not to look in West Virginia. Typically when someone goes into WITSEC the Feds move them out of the area so no one accidentally recognizes them. They're probably living in a big city where they can blend in. It's possible they're using the same first names though. It's common for people in the program to keep their same first names, or at least their initials, so they don't make some stupid mistake when introducing themselves."

"You think they're in the same city?"

"Doubtful. They might be in the same state. That might make it easier for the Marshals to keep an eye on them, but they wouldn't want one bumping into the other. If these two guys got a deal, there would be conditions."

"Like what?"

"The usual stuff. They can't go back home. No contact with family or friends. No contact with each other. Definitely no contact with the victim's family. Basically, they have to avoid anything that could blow their cover."

"Anyone ever been found once they went into the program?"

He laughed. "I know you get a boner about going after these types of marks, but you've got an uphill battle here, my friend. I know WITSEC pretty well, and no one who has followed the rules has ever been found. Now, you've always got some stupid asshole mobster who outs himself—moves back to his hometown or calls his mother or something. Those guys don't last too long. Last year there was a girl, maybe twenty-three or four, who went into the program after testifying against her husband, who was some big-time gang leader in Miami. The Feds shipped her off to Minnesota. Guess the cold got to her, because she lost it and moved back to Miami after only a few months. Cops pulled her out of a Waffle House dumpster two days after she showed up in town. That sort of thing. But the people who take it seriously, the ones who keep their head down and their mouth shut, they disappear, man. No one's ever been found."

"But someone has to know where these people are. There has to be some sort of database. Something tying their real identifies to their fake ones?"

"I'm sure the CIA has documents identifying their deep cover operatives too, but it doesn't mean you're gonna find it."

"What about agents on the inside? Would it be possible to get someone to turn and give up their new identities or hack into a database and find them?"

"Not likely. You're dealing with a very small team of people. There might only be two or three agents who know their exact locations. They do it that way so some dirty LEO can't compromise the asset. They even use different computer systems so marshals outside the team can't access key details. It's solid all around. You're going to need a lot of luck on this one."

I swirled my hand and watched the inky coffee cascade off the side of the porcelain cup.

"If you were me where would you start?"

"I'd start by shaving. That beard looks like shit."

I didn't say anything as I ran my fingers across my finely trimmed chin and smiled wide enough for him to see my molars.

"I'd start with their relatives," he continued. "Maybe you'll get lucky and one of these two is talking to someone he's not supposed to be talking to. You're looking for a needle in a Goddamn haystack, man."

"What about drawing them out of hiding? Make them come to me. Like you said, the ones who get caught usually do something stupid. Maybe I can get them to poke their head out of the rabbit's hole."

"It's much easier to make people disappear than it is to find them. But, if I was trying to do it, that's probably the approach I'd take. Draw them out, or start with the parents or siblings since those are tough relationships to sever. Maybe a girlfriend. When these people do get discovered, it's because they did something stupid. It's hard to stay under, man. Real hard. Especially if you've got family on the outside. The first thing I do with my clients before we do anything else is make sure they're really ready to go under. Most of them just want a fresh start and have no idea what it really entails."

"Anyone ever find one of your clients?"

"Fuck no! That'd be bad for business. I did have one guy, a CEO who was running from the IRS a few years ago, he did a few stupid things and I had to make him realize there were consequences for his actions. After we had a little chat he went back under and I haven't had any problems with him since."

I tossed the rest of the coffee down my throat and set the empty mug on the desk next to the coffee pot. "Thanks. I appreciate your help."

"Sorry I couldn't help more. I wish you the best of luck, man. You'll need it. And more."

I shook his hand and turned for the door.

"Look, Finn, I know I'm not going to dissuade you, but

remember the Feds want these guys buried. They've probably spent a lot of time, effort and money to hide them. You start poking around too deep and you might draw some unwanted attention."

"I'm hoping I get the attention."

"Why's that?"

"Because I'll know I'm close. Maybe someone pops up and leads me right to them."

"That's not a bad idea. Both of these guys are going to have a contact on the inside, probably with the Marshals Service. Figure out who the contact is and you might be able to track them that way." He laughed. "But seriously, lose the beard."

I slid the pocket doors open and then turned back.

"One last question," I said.

"What's that?"

"What's it like having your mother work for you?"

"Shit, man. Not as bad as you might think. She loves to work, keeps the place super clean and makes lunch. It keeps her mind sharp too. Best secretary I've ever had."

"Assistant!" the woman yelled from a back room.

"Right. Assistant. It's good, man. It's not like I live with her or anything. That would be weird."

I thought about my father. He had probably finished his *Columbo* marathon and moved on to *Quincy M.E.* reruns. "Right. That would be weird."

I grabbed a red-and-white mint from the lobby and returned to my car.

CHAPTER 7

SOMETHING GYPSY SCOTT said unnerved me. He said no one in WITSEC who followed the rules had ever been found. That didn't surprise me because the government needed the WITSEC program to work. It has to be effective, because if anyone broke through the carefully crafted misinformation barriers and got to someone on the inside Uncle Sam would have a hard time persuading others to enter the program. If the DOJ could not guarantee protection the program would crumble into nothingness.

One thing in my favor was that it was difficult to follow the rules. New name, new location, new car, new job, new hobbies, new language patterns, new everything. Imagine having to completely disconnect from your life. No contact with parents, friends, coworkers—all the people we look to when things go to shit. Everything you ever knew has to become a memory. Even people in the program who know someone is actively looking to kill them have trouble remaining under.

I wondered if I could stay under completely, if I could sever ties with my family and give up everything and everyone I knew. I'm not sure I could do it, even with the threat of a bullet, or in Willie Baker's case a hammer, to the head.

The DOJ designed WITSEC to protect mob informants and others who knew once they testified their lives would be in danger. It wasn't a possibility, it was a certainty. That wasn't the case with Vance and Turner. They weren't actively evading anyone. They entered protection *in case* someone came looking for them, but the probability of that happening was low. Besides Willie Baker's failed PIs and me, I doubt anyone ever came looking for them.

Another factor in my favor was the length of time Vance and Turner had been under. They disappeared two-and-a-half decades ago and that meant they were complacent. I imagine when they first arrived in their new locations with their new identities they followed the rules of protection to the letter. As time slipped by they eased up. It's human nature. They got more comfortable and did things they weren't supposed to do. Maybe they called someone they should stay away from. Maybe they went somewhere they were not supposed to go. Maybe it was a drunken email or telling purchase. Something as simple as a crinkled birthday card in the garbage can could lead to something. The clues would be there. They would be subtle, but they would be there.

Finding those who don't want to be found comes down to paperwork. Ninety percent of what I do is research, or "ass time." That's where the details are. Where the real information is. Albert would never see Lieutenant Columbo sitting at his desk reviewing phone records, court transcripts or property records. That's not interesting and it makes for shitty television. But that's also where the answers are and that's where I began looking for Vance and Turner.

For me the first part of any investigation is the workup. It is mind-numbingly boring. But it's important and it informs everything else I'll do to find these two. Somewhere in this blur of information is a kernel that will point me in the direction I need to go, like a dowsing rod. A breadcrumb that will lead me to another, and another and right to Vance's and Turner's front doors. It'll show me the way, and if I follow it correctly I'll find them. Both of them.

Contrary to what Gypsy Scott might tell his clients, it's impossible to disappear. All you can do it throw up roadblocks, smoke and mirrors and hope whoever is looking for you gets tired or has something else better to do with their time. I made a living out of leaping roadblocks and not following smoke or mirrors. If Vance and Turner were alive and still in the country, I would find them. It could be a long journey, but the first step was the profile.

For the next week I found everything I could on Vance's and Turner's backgrounds and families. When I finished I had a thick white binder full of data, separated by colorful tabs that would make an anal-retentive accountant squeal like Ned Beatty.

Information on Jacob Vance and Ray Turner was limited because they spent a big chunk of their young lives in juvenile detention before going into protection. They didn't have bank accounts, social security activity, employment records, assets or credit cards. There was little associated with their birth names, but they did have parents. And mommy and daddy had their own digital footprints, which were available if you knew where to look. And I knew where to look.

The first half of my binder included everything I found on Thomas and Theresa Vance, Jacob Vance's parents. Both were still alive and living outside Parkersburg. By rummaging through a variety of databases and making a few calls to Cricket I'd compiled everything I could on the Vance ecosystem. I had social security information, tax records, employment histories, financial details, asset and property records, motor vehicle registrations, phone records, information on business associates, criminal records, insurance policies, and medical records.

All this information gave me an idea of who Thomas and Theresa Vance were. Credit card transactions revealed the Vances ordered pizza from a local pizzeria every Friday night and that their favorite charity was the Humane Society. I knew that they'd paid for their current house in cash, Thomas spent a few hundred bucks a month at the Wheeling Island Casino, and Theresa suffered from proliferative retinopathy, a diabetic eye disease, and took corticosteroids as part of her treatment. I also knew Jacob Vance had a sister, Debra, who worked at a local car dealership and recently gave birth to a daughter, Emily, who weighed six-and-a-half pounds.

Some of this information might seem mundane, but I had to be thorough. Property records might reveal a rental unit or vacation home where Jacob could frequent. Medical records might indicate a rare hereditary disease that could lead me to a medical support group or tip me off to a certain medication Jacob might be taking. Phone records could reveal frequent out-of-state telephone calls. The birth of a niece could bring Jacob out of hiding for a visit with his sister, or a maybe he sent a gift with his address on it. They were all small possibilities, but I had to investigate every angle.

The second part of my big-ass binder focused on Ray Turner. That section was much thinner compared to Vance's workup because the Turners were dirt-poor and long dead, so there wasn't much in the way of useful information. No bank accounts, investments, assets or property. Bruce Turner clocked out twelve years ago from a brain aneurism and his wife, Denise, followed a few months later by way of a tailpipe, a garden hose and an idling pickup truck. Except for their burial plots in the same cemetery where Josh Baker was buried, there were few traces of their existence.

A review of birth records turned up no Turner siblings, so while I wasn't back to square one, I was damn close. Unlike Vance's workup, Turner's gave me little to work with and that made me nervous. Gathering any additional information on Bruce or Denise Turner would require a shovel and the cover of darkness, so I decided to focus my investigation on Jacob Vance first and hope that finding him might point me in Raymond Turner's direction. It was possible Vance and Turner were still in touch, and if I could find one he might lead me to the other.

Background research is vital in a case like this, but so is the human element. Someone out there knew where Vance and Turner called home and I had to find them. My gut told me Vance's parents knew where he was. They wouldn't tell me, of course, but I could still use them as a compass to find magnetic north.

I flipped to the last part of my binder and thumbed through the newspaper coverage from the boys' trial. Nell Richards, a reporter from the *Parkersburg Sentinel*, filed several articles during the trial, but a quick search revealed she hadn't written anything about the case since 1985.

Journalists can be a gold mine of information. Their brains are wired to remember things most people forget. Nell Richards was my first stop on the Josh Baker Express. Next stop, Parkersburg, West Virginia.

CHAPTER 8

NELL RICHARDS LIVED in a modest home a few miles outside Parkersburg. It was a nice neighborhood, the kind of place where you expect to see kids riding their bikes, climbing trees and playing kickball in the street.

I grabbed my notebook, picked up the newspaper waiting at the end of her driveway and walked to the front door. I knocked and a moment later she opened the door wide without checking to see who had done the knocking. Nell was a black woman in her early sixties. She had honest eyes and short dark hair with streaks of gray throughout. She was dressed like she had been to church.

"Ms. Richards?" I said, handing her the newspaper.

She looked me up and down. "I'm not used to having strange men on my porch."

"My name is Roger Mathers. I'm an author and I was hoping you had a few minutes to talk about the Josh Baker case."

She stepped back, and from the look on her face I thought she might slam the door in my bearded face.

"Say that again," she said.

"The Josh Baker case." I held up my notebook as if proof that I was legit. "I was hoping you had some time to answer a few questions about it."

She didn't say anything, but I could tell she was trying to figure out why a man she'd never seen before was standing on her front porch asking questions about a thirty-two-year-old murder. After a moment, she stepped aside and motioned me in.

"Mr. Mathers you said?"

"That's right."

She ushered me through her living room and into her kitchen, where she pulled out a chair for me at a small round kitchen table. "Have a seat."

Framed pages from the *Parkersburg Sentinel* lined her kitchen walls. Black and white snapshots provided a timeline of local history from the Massey Energy Big Branch coal mine explosion, a crippling snow storm, a mine collapse that killed a dozen miners, and Senator Robert Byrd's death, among other events.

I sat down and crossed my legs. "You covered the Baker case for the local paper?" I said.

"I did." She took a seat across from me. "I'm a small-town girl, Mr. Mathers, which means I'll extend a seat at my table to pretty much anyone. How long you're welcome to sit there depends on you."

"I understand, and thanks for speaking with me."

"Can I offer you a drink? Coffee? Tea?"

I wanted a cup of coffee, but the coffeemaker on her countertop was empty and I needed information more than caffeine.

"No, thank you."

"I'm curious, Mr. Mathers." She rubbed her chin. "Why are you digging up ghosts?"

"I'm writing a book on the case. A look back after thirty-two years."

"It's going to be a short book," she said. "You've got a dead boy and two murderers who disappeared into thin air."

"That's what I wanted to talk to you about. I'd like…" I paused, not sure I wanted to tip my hand yet.

She saw through me. "You're trying to find them."

I nodded.

"Best of luck to you. You'd have an easier time finding an honest politician." She laughed at her joke. "Those two are as good as gone and I don't think they'll ever come back."

"That's what I figured, and it's also why I'm here. I'm hoping you could give me a push in the right direction, considering these two could be anywhere."

"I'm sorry to disappoint you, but I don't think I can be much help. I covered the trial through the verdict, but that was it. Never really spoke of it again."

"You never thought of a follow-up piece?"

"Sure, I thought about it all right. Took the idea to my editor several times to get the green light. Everyone round here wanted to know what happened to those two, but it got shot down."

"Why's that?"

"Gag order. Everything about the case is sealed. Our paper is a small operation and we could barely make enough in advertising to cover printing most of the time. The boss wasn't about to risk a big fine and maybe even a lawsuit for breaking that order."

"You were the crime reporter at the paper?"

"Right. Covered some other beats too, but mostly crime."

"You got a lot of crime around here to write about?"

"Not really. I managed the police blotter section. Breaking and entering, drunks fighting with one another, but nothing like the Baker case. That hit this town like a tornado. Stirred up a bunch of shit in its wake too."

"What do you mean?"

"People started to look at each other differently, you know? Everyone was a lot more suspicious of their neighbors and the kids down the street. The loners who stuck out as a little weird."

"Like Vance and Turner?"

"Right. This is a small town and we weren't prepared for something like that. Horrible mess it was. And then to have them get out and get new identities and all. A lot of people were pissed off about that."

"Did you write about that? About the new identities?"

"Didn't need to. Like I said, it's a small town. People talk."

"You ever hear of anything like that before?" I said. "The government assigning new identities like they did?"

"Nothing like this. Those two had someone looking out for them. Had to. Otherwise they would have done their time and been released just like everyone else."

"Any idea who might have helped them?"

"I've got my suspicions."

I leaned in close. "Care to share?"

"Jacob Vance. His father, Thomas, was on the city council in eighty-three. I did some research over the years. Thought I might write a book about it someday. Like you. Turns out Thomas Vance worked his way from councilman all the way up to the Department of Justice. He wasn't a bigwig there by any means, but the connection alone made me suspicious. He could have known someone who knew someone who could have got those kids a deal. I don't know. There's nothing official, just the hunch of an old reporter."

I scribbled her theory in my pad. "Sounds like a solid hunch."

She shrugged.

"But wouldn't a scandal like that—your kid killing someone—pretty much ruin a political career?"

"It did," she said. "He served out his term on the council and then he was done. He still worked for the government, but never again as an elected official."

"What did he do?"

"Went to work for the DOJ in Washington."

"That's pretty big time."

"I guess. I think I remember him doing something with computers. Computer forensics maybe?"

"What about the mother?"

"Nothing remarkable that stood out to me. I know she visited her son quite a bit at the juvenile detention center, several times a week. She was also at the trial every day. The other parents too. They didn't grant me any interviews even though I asked. Several times. I can't imagine what they went through. Knowing your kid did something like that and having to live with it forever." She shook her head.

"Anything stand out with Turner's parents?"

"Not that I can remember. There wasn't a bright spotlight on them. Not like today where you blame the parents for everything. Back then they seemed like victims themselves. As if their own children had been taken away from them. And I guess they had. If Vance and Turner are in some sort of protection, who knows, maybe they aren't allowed to see their parents. That's got to be hard on their mothers and fathers. To go through that. I'm not saying they have it as bad as Willie Baker, of course not, but as a mother myself, your heart breaks for everyone involved."

"Anything else you can think of that could help me figure out a path to Vance or Turner? Anything you came across in the reporting."

"I had a contact inside the detention center where the boys were held." She thought for a moment. "Daniel Schuster. He was a security guard. I didn't get a lot of traction from it, but I met with him a few times to learn about their life on the inside. Until the paper squashed the story anyway. He's retired now and he might talk to you. He thought Vance and Turner got off way too easy."

"Doesn't everyone?"

"That trial had this whole town up in arms. There was a lot more to it than just the crime and the verdict. Some people were screaming for Vance's and Turner's heads, but there was another side to it. Those two boys were tried as adults and a lot of people thought that shouldn't have happened even though they were disgusted by the murder. It was really strange to think of two nine year olds…" She stopped. "Actually, they both turned ten before the trial. Strange to see two ten year olds sitting in that courtroom. Between us, I think them being tried as adults helped get them the anonymity deal. Maybe someone in the DOJ thought they should have never been in that courtroom in the first place and this was their way of making it right."

"Why were they tried as adults? Nine years old seems like a stretch."

"I guess because some shrink thought the boys knew what they were doing was wrong. That was enough to get them a seat in big-boy court."

"I'm sure the shit hit the fan with the verdict."

"It did. It was a real big deal around here. People standing outside the courtroom cheering. I think the entire town was happy with the verdict, even though there was some contention on whether they should have been tried as adults. Lot of folk here have children of their own and all they had to do was think about their kids in little Josh's place and... Well, everyone was happy to see them found guilty. There was no question those two were responsible."

"What about the sentence?"

"That was a slap in the face. I was a crime reporter, not a legal scholar, but to me it seemed way too light. I think it was their age again. Had they been adults, they'd still be locked up."

I tapped my pen on my notepad. "You were at the trial?"

"Every day."

"Was any evidence presented on who actually killed Josh? I read that Vance and Turner each blamed each other, but was it ever proven who actually killed Josh?"

"I don't recall. Neither Vance nor Turner took the stand at trial so there was no he-said-he-said going on. There was a psychologist who testified to the boys' state of mind. I interviewed him and I remember him saying something about one of the boys being more of a leader and probably coercing the other along, but I don't recall the specifics. All that would be in my notes. Those are probably locked in the paper's archives, if they haven't already pitched them. If my notes would be helpful I can see about getting them. I've still got a lot of friends at the paper."

"What about Vance's father? You ever follow up on that hunch?"

"He's not going to talk to anyone about his son, and I really don't want to make enemies with anyone connected to the DOJ. Maybe if I was younger and more ambitious but not now. I don't need that kind of trouble."

"You still do work for the paper?"

"Hell no." She ran a hand through her hair. "See this gray? The paper did that. I've been retired for five years."

"Why not write that book then?"

"I considered it, but there's too much red tape. I'd never get the information I needed. Most of the people who were involved are long gone, and with no access to Vance or Turner all I could do is recap the articles I wrote thirty years ago." She smiled. "Plus I'd have to compete with your book, and you look like you know what you're doing." She stood up. "Let me give you Daniel's number. I've got it on my computer."

Nell disappeared into a back bedroom and returned a minute later with a red folder.

"Here are most of the articles I filed on the case. You're welcome to these if they'll help. Without the legal briefs and police reports you're not going to get much detail, and those are all sealed."

"I have the case file."

She crossed her arms. "How'd you get that? It's supposed to be sealed."

"I know someone who knows someone."

"Like I said, you look like you know what you're doing."

I nodded.

"Well, you've already gotten farther than I did," she said. "I was in the courtroom when we heard a lot of that information but I couldn't report all of it." She pointed to the folder. "Daniel's name and number are on the front there. Last I spoke with him was about four years ago when I was considering the book. No telling if the number is still active or if he's even still alive."

I took the folder.

"My number is on there too. I doubt I can help you much, but I'll help any way I can. The only two people who can give you any real information are hiding out behind new names and adult faces. I really hope you find those two though, and I hope they talk to you. I'm dying to know what happened to them. Maybe it will offer everyone some closure."

"Thanks. I'll be sure to include you in the acknowledgements of my book."

"Don't bother. This case stunk from day one and it continues to stink today. The crime itself was unsettling enough, but to know those two kids are all grown up out there enjoying their lives. A lot of people don't like it. They could be anywhere. I'll help you all I can, which probably won't be much since I don't know anything I haven't already written about. But I don't want my name out there. No telling what could happen."

She walked me to the door.

"Normally I'd tell you to try the parents, but the Turners are both dead and I don't think you're going to get much out of the Vances. They didn't talk back then and I doubt they'll talk now. The last thing they're gonna want is someone dredging all this up again. Bringing their boy back into the spotlight."

"Thanks for all your help, Nell."

She patted me on the shoulder. "Can't say I agree with what you're doing or not. Sometimes it's just best to let ghosts be.

Nothing you or I could write is going to bring that little boy any justice. He lost that a long time ago."

"I understand your point, but something is pushing me forward to write this book. Or at least research it. Who knows, it might all fall apart."

"I hope you don't run into problems. Trouble with the government and all. They put those boys in hiding and I suspect they'll want to keep them there."

I cracked a smile. "Nell, I'm pretty much expecting trouble." I reached into my pocket and handed her a business card. "If you think of anything else that would be helpful could you give me a call?"

"Sure." She studied the card. "Like I said, don't expect much from me, but I'll see what I can do."

I thanked her and walked across the front porch. She waited for me to get into my car before she closed the door.

CHAPTER 9

IN MY CAR I flipped through the red folder Nell gave me. At first glance the articles looked like the ones I'd found while researching the case. I would study them closer when I had more time. Now I was more interested in what Daniel Schuster might have to tell me about Vance and Turner. Since he was on the inside with them he might be able to tell me something about their life and habits at Pleasant Hill. Something they might have continued on the outside.

I called Daniel and told him I had spoken with Nell and hoped to meet him in person to learn more about his interactions with Vance and Turner. I kept up the author backstory since most people love to talk to authors, and I hoped Daniel was no different. He agreed to see me at his place. I punched his address into my GPS and twenty minutes later I pulled through the gates of his neighborhood.

He lived in a retirement community, but it wasn't one of those typical old-folks communities. In this neighborhood each resident had a two-bedroom unit, a single-car garage and a small, neatly manicured lawn that was probably managed by a landscaping company. Each bungalow was a different color, each brighter than the last. Lots of yellows, blues and oranges. It reminded me of the beach homes I've seen in the Bahamas and those afternoon television commercials for retirement communities in Florida, minus the golf courses and swimming pools. I'd made a mental note of those places should Albert become intolerable.

Daniel Schuster met me on the front porch of his bright blue bungalow. He looked as though he'd been waiting for me, as if he wanted to be outside when I arrived. Daniel looked to be in his seventies. He wore a thick jacket that was too heavy for the brisk November weather and he smelled like the barbershop Albert took me to as a kid.

"Mr. Schuster?" I said, hoping he would tell me to call him Dan. He didn't.

"That's right. You the writer that called?"

"Yessir. Roger Mathers." I reached out my hand. "Nell suggested I chat with you."

He shook it without standing up from his porch chair. "You can drop the sir. You don't work for me." He sized me up. "You spoke with Nell, huh? She don't put up with much shit. So if she told you to call me I guess you're okay." He looked at the notebook in my hand. "A writer, huh? What you write'n?"

"I'm researching a book on Jacob Vance and Ray Turner. And the Josh Baker murder."

He nodded. "Well I don't know how I can help you with that. That was a long time ago."

"Nell said you worked at Pleasant Hill when Vance and Turner were there. That you were a guard."

"Patient advisor," he said. "They called us patient advisors not guards, even though that's what we were."

"Do you remember interacting with them?"

"Yeah. Saw them both."

"What were they like?"

"Just like everyone else there I guess. Didn't come off as cold-blooded killers. Kept to themselves mostly. Pretty quiet kids. Stuck to the rules and blended in. Not much trouble that I remember."

"Did they see each other on the inside?"

"No. They were on separate floors and weren't allowed to move about much. I worked all the floors though. All us guards rotated each day. That's how I got to know them both. What kind of information you looking for?"

He motioned to a second porch chair and I sat down and leaned forward, my notepad on my knee.

"The guards, you guys talk at all? Maybe hear something about where Vance and Turner went once they got out?"

"You asking if I know where they are?"

"Yeah. I want to talk to them about the case. Now that so much time has gone by, I want to give them the chance to tell their story."

"Shit, son. Those boys are long gone. The bureaucrats saw to that."

"Anything you can tell me to help locate them?"

"That's a fool's errand. If I hear it right, they ain't the type of people you find."

"How's that?"

He searched his jacket pocket for something but gave up. "They got protection. Disappeared." He adjusted his porch chair and leaned back. "You know they only did eight years for that murder? And not a minute of it in prison. That's what really bothers me. They didn't spend a single day in prison. Did their entire time at Pleasant Hill. It's no country club, but it ain't no jail neither. They probably lived better than half of West Virginia. Meals cooked for them, got to watch television whenever they wanted, education classes. How's that punishment? Christ, one of 'em even had a girlfriend."

My eyes narrowed. I snatched my pad from my lap and clicked open my pen. "What do you mean a girlfriend?"

"Turner. I think it was Turner." He paused. "Yeah, it was Turner. He had a girlfriend. Kim something. I can't remember her last name."

I wrote her name on my pad. "This girlfriend, she come to visit him while he was inside?"

"No, she was a patient there too. She was older than him by a year or two. Pleasant Hill was a coed facility, but the patients were segregated by floor. She wasn't supposed to be up on our floor, but she got up there anyway. If I saw her I'd send her packing, but some of the other guards, they let her be. She'd flash them her titties and they'd look the other way. I never asked her to do that."

"And you don't remember her last name? Just Kim."

He thought again. "Sorry. All I can remember is Kim."

"Was it serious? Their relationship?"

"I don't know. They were around each other a lot. I mean as much as they could be with us guards and all. I probably saw them together once a week. We all knew they were messing around. I guess no one cared. Like I said, I'd tell her to get lost, but I wasn't always around."

"When was this? How old was Turner?"

"Probably sixteen. Think they were still seeing each other when they let him out at eighteen. She was still there for a few months after he got out."

"What about Vance? He have a girlfriend too?"

Daniel shook his head and grimaced like he didn't want to talk to me anymore. "Not that I recall. I do remember his parents came to visit a lot though. Not every day, but a few times a week. They always brought him cupcakes. I remember that. It seemed like they were really close. I know if I did what he did my parents would have whipped and disowned me, not brought me cupcakes."

"Who came to see him? His mother or father? Or both?"

"Mostly his mother. She was there a lot. I'm sure his father came too, but not as often as his mother. She was there enough that I thought it was strange."

"Why was it strange?"

"With most of those kids, when they first came in their parents would come once a week. Then it tapered to once every two weeks and sometimes once a month, but she came all the time. It never dwindled."

"What about Turner's parents? They come to visit?"

"I'm sure they did, but it wasn't a regular thing. Not like Vance. You might be able to look at the logbooks at Pleasant Hill and see how often they came by. I know it was a lot for Vance."

"Anything else you can tell me that might help me find Vance or Turner? Anything, even something small that might push me in the right direction?"

"I'm sorry, son. You got to understand it was a long time ago and I think everyone in this town wanted to forget about those boys. Me included." He scratched his head. "You could contact Pleasant Hill. Maybe find someone else on the staff who was there with Vance and Turner. I know they met with doctors as part of their treatment, so maybe there's a lead there. I just don't have anything for you." He stood up indicting the conversation was over. "I don't know what else to tell you. I don't know how you could find them. But if you do, I hope you find them dead. And I don't feel bad about saying that. I'm a Christian and I believe everyone should get a second chance, but what they did to that boy… it wasn't human."

I stood up and shook his hand. "Thanks for your time." I stepped off the porch as Daniel searched an inside pocket for whatever he didn't find in his front pockets. I had one foot in my Navigator when he shouted at me.

"Burton!"

"What?" I said, turning.

"Kim Burton. The girlfriend. Burton."

"You've been a big help, Daniel. Thank you." I waved as he disappeared back into his blue bungalow.

I sat in the driver's seat and wondered how likely it was that Kim Burton had had any contact with Turner after being released. Gypsy Scott said people who went under had a hard time severing ties with the outside world. That made sense. I'd bet that at some point, after a certain amount of time, everyone who went under thought about coming up to see a loved one. They probably rationalized how much harm they could do by making one phone call or sending an email. The fact that Kim and Turner spent some time together at Pleasant Hill meant they had some connection. Two years is enough time to create a strong bond, and while I'm no shrink, I'd imagine Turner was probably the type of person who didn't connect with a lot of people.

For Vance, I'd go after his parents since they were the best link in his tether to the surface. But for Turner, all I had was a girlfriend who would do anything, like lift her shirt to the prison guards, to see him. If she still had that fierce dedication maybe I could use her to get to him.

CHAPTER 10

That Theresa Vance visited her son at Pleasant Hill several times a week, and even brought cupcakes, told me they had a strong relationship. A strange one maybe, but strong nonetheless. I hoped their relationship endured through his new identity.

I did not find anything in my workup that connected Theresa to her son. No regular bank transfers, no telephone records indicating a relationship with someone on the other side of the country, nothing that led me straight to him, but I had a hunch there was something there. That meant staking out the Vance homestead waiting for anything that offered a connection to Jacob. I'd sit on the home for a few days until I established a pattern of activity. Once I was certain Theresa and Thomas would be out of the home, I would go in and try to find something to get me closer to Jacob.

I hated stakeouts. They are worse than anal fissures and church. It doesn't matter how much you accomplish sitting in a comfortable office with your feet up on the desk, do this job long enough and at some point you will find yourself in a cramped car in the middle of the night fighting sleep and boredom waiting for something to happen.

Stakeouts aren't like the movies. The big screen never shows the detectives driving around to find the right secluded location to watch their mark, being hunched over in the driver's seat for seven hours at a time suffering through back spasms and cramps, pissing in bottles or explaining to an observant police officer what in the hell they were doing in a strange neighborhood at three in the morning. Ninety-nine percent of stakeouts is sitting in a car twiddling your thumbs for hours watching nothing happen. Nothing. But as shitty as they are, staking out a location or an individual can get you intel you won't find elsewhere. Just like dumpster diving, the dirtiest methods often yield the best results. Sometimes you just have to hold your breath and dive in.

The last two cases I worked had tight deadlines. The kind of deadlines that when missed meant someone ended up with more holes in their body than God intended. This case was different. Since I did not have a gun to my head I could take my time and conduct a proper investigation. An investigation that allowed for a few nights of stakeouts. That's another thing Hollywood gets wrong. Nothing exciting ever happens the first night of a stakeout. Ever.

I arrived at the Vances' house at eight o'clock on a Saturday evening. Jacob Vance's parents lived ten miles outside Parkersburg in an unassuming two-story home on Linden Drive. They had a two-car garage, four floodlights bolted to the sides of the home and a surveillance camera over the front door. From my parking spot about fifty yards away I had a clear view of the front of the house. The curtains were pulled tight, but there were several lights on inside.

As I watched the house my thoughts turned to my workup binder. I grabbed it from the passenger seat and traded glances between the black-and-white pages and the house far off in front of me.

Nell Richards was right. Thomas Vance had a career in government. My research corroborated he had been a council member in Parkersburg in the early ‘80s, then moved to the United States Attorney's office in West Virginia and finally to the Department of Justice in Washington, D.C. before retiring immediately after his sixty-first birthday. He never worked on the legal side at either the Attorney's office or the DOJ. He ran technology programs. According to Theresa's employment record, she switched jobs every few years and now worked at a local real estate agency.

I flipped to anther section of the binder and reviewed a series of police reports the Vances had filed over the years. Theresa had filed more than a dozen reports against individuals for vandalism and trespassing, most of which coincided with her son's release in 1992. Apparently some locals were unhappy with the release, and since they couldn't take it out on Jacob Vance they turned to his parents.

Auditor records showed Thomas and Theresa Vance had moved six times since their son's release. At first I was surprised they had not left the state to get a fresh start somewhere else, but their daughter also lived near Parkersburg so it made sense that Thomas and Theresa stayed nearby to be a part of her and her family's life. Since the daughter had married and taken her husband's last name, she had probably been spared the stigma of being a Vance.

I looked back at the house and watched the downstairs lights click off one by one and then a moment later an upstairs light, likely in a bedroom, clicked on. Two hours later someone snuffed that light out and the entire house fell dark.

After another hour I pulled out of the subdivision and found an all-night diner for a quick bite before checking into a roadside motel and paying more than I should for a hard mattress, a thick pillow and a leaky faucet. It could have been the lack of sleep and a preference for paranoia, but I was certain a silver SUV followed me half the way to the motel, but it pulled off the main road before I made it to the parking lot.

Before I fell asleep that night I thought about Willie Baker and how he got a raw deal. Not as raw as his son got, but he still ended up on the wrong end of life's toilet plunger. I tried to imagine what he went through. First to learn his son was missing and then to have hope immediately turn to grief when the police found Josh's body. Then the agony of reliving his son's murder during the trial and finally watching the two responsible walk out free men after serving only eight years. Those experiences rob the life out of you and make swallowing a gun seem like a good escape.

I WOKE UP AT 7:00 A.M., GRABBED A SHOWER AND BREAKFAST AND was back in front of Thomas and Theresa's house an hour later. I didn't like watching the place in the daylight, but I had nothing else to do. Jacob Vance's parents were the only leads I had for him, and I had to sit on them until they led me somewhere. I had only been there forty-five minutes when the garage door opened and a black Jeep Grand Cherokee rolled out of the garage and turned down the street. Time to see where it took me.

I gave the Jeep enough distance and then pulled out behind it. I followed it out of their neighborhood and onto Route 14. After about ten miles it pulled into a strip mall parking lot on the right side of the street. I took the next right and circled the block. I drove past the strip mall and pulled into a supermarket next to the parking lot where the black Jeep sat empty.

A few businesses lined the strip mall, but I was interested in the one on the far end, Kichurchak and Associates. That was the name on Theresa Vance's employment record. I wasn't going to start asking Theresa questions about Jacob, because the last thing I wanted was her knowing someone was looking for her son, but I did want to see her. I wanted to put a human face on this case and that started with her.

I left my Navigator, crossed the parking lot and pulled on the glass door, but it was locked. Looking up, I saw a woman walking toward me. She checked her watch, unlocked the door and opened it a few inches.

"Can I help you?"

"I wanted to speak with a realtor about finding a property," I said.

She checked her watch again. Her shoulders relaxed as if she was less nervous now than when she opened the door.

"We don't open for another ten minutes, but I guess we could start a bit earlier today."

"Are you sure? I can come back."

"No, that's silly," she said. "Come on in."

She opened the door wide and stepped aside. Kichurchak and Associates had a small office. Four cubicles stood on each side of the room and two conferences tables were in the back next to a larger office, maybe for a director or executive. This wasn't the kind of real estate company where the agents wore gold jackets and plastered their faces on bus stop benches. As I followed the woman to her cubicle I scanned the nameplates on the other cubicle partitions. Each plastic nameplate featured the realtor's first and last name, except for the one I walked toward. This one had a first name but only the last initial. Theresa V. Not surprising, because who wants to buy a house from the mother of a child killer?

"Have a seat," she said, motioning to two small chairs inside the gray partition.

I pulled the seat away from her desk and sat down. My back hit the cubicle wall.

"Are you local?"

I felt like she was feeling me out. A local might know her or know she was Jacob Vance's mother.

"No. From Cincinnati," I said. "Roger Mathers."

"Theresa Vance." She sounded uncomfortable, like she wasn't used to saying her name out loud.

I reached across the desk and shook her hand, wondering if she would have shared her last name had I said I was from Parkersburg.

Theresa had wiry gray hair. She was short and thin and looked like she hadn't eaten in days. When we shook hands the gold bracelet on her right wrist slid all the way to her elbow and I half expected it to slip off her arm when I released my grip.

I leaned back in the chair and crossed my legs. I wasn't sure if I was supposed to feel empathy for this woman or something else. After all, her nine-year-old son murdered a four-year-old boy in cold blood. No motive, no nothing. That had to come from somewhere. I know there is evil in the world, but I also know evil doesn't suddenly manifest itself overnight. I have dealt with a lot of killers, but they all killed for a reason. Money, revenge, power. But Vance and Turner killed a helpless boy for no reason at all. Was this woman who sat across from me responsible for the monster Jacob Vance became, or was there more to it?

"So you're looking for a property here in Parkersburg?"

"Yes." I tried to forget for a moment that I had been hired to track down her son knowing that someone else would cave his head in with a hammer.

"What brings you here? From Cincinnati."

"My wife and I are looking for something we can use as an investment property. Something we could rent out. Maybe near the WVU Parkersburg campus."

She nodded. "I think I might be able to help." She struggled to pull a thick white binder from the storage cabinet affixed to her cubicle wall.

For the next fifteen minutes I watched as she flipped through laminated pages showing me photos of one and two-bedroom houses. Part of me didn't want to be sitting there because I was making this too personal, but on some level I wanted to know who she was and I needed more than what my research binder gave me. My daughter, Becca, was eight years old—only one year younger than Vance when he helped murder Josh Baker—and I felt some distant connection with Theresa, a connection as a parent who wanted only the best for their kid. For her, that hope vanished like a sidewalk chalk sketch in the rain.

"So what do you think?" she said. "Any of these properties strike an interest?"

I looked down at the mosaic of photos in front of me. "Yes, a few of them look really nice. I think I'd like to bring my wife in as a next step. So we can look at potential properties together."

"That's a lovely idea." She slipped her business card from a plastic holder and handed it to me. "My hours are on the back. Give me a call whenever you're ready to sit down and talk further."

I tucked the card inside my wallet. "I'll do that. Thank you, Theresa." I shook her hand again, and for the first time she smiled. I stood and walked out of her office knowing that if I ever saw her again it would be from inside my car, fifty yards away.

CHAPTER 11

THAT EVENING I drove back to the Vance house and took my usual spot on the street. Besides Thomas Vance wheeling two garbage cans to the curb, nothing happened.

Nothing until 8:45 p.m., when Theresa walked out of the front door onto the porch. I grabbed my binoculars from the console. She was dressed like someone who went into a sporting goods store, plunked down a credit card and said, "Make me look like a runner." I watched as she walked to the sidewalk, stared down the street and then bent over to stretch. She stood up, turned to check the other side of the street and then stretched again. Then she jogged down the street toward the intersection of Linden Drive and Cypress Way.

Normally, someone going for a nighttime jog didn't raise a red flag, but then I remembered the medical record in my workup. Theresa Vance suffered from a diabetic eye disease, the same eye disease that my mother had. My mother took a corticosteroid, as Theresa does, to slow the progression, but she was not supposed to exert herself—that meant no running. And someone as thin as Theresa Vance didn't need to jog to manage her weight. That made it suspicious.

I had to tail her, but that meant leaving the car. The darkness provided enough cover to slip through the neighborhood unnoticed, but I didn't like the scenario. Someone out walking a dog or dragging a garbage can to the curb could expose me, and the echo of my boots pounding down the sidewalk could attract more attention than I wanted.

I didn't have another option. Theresa Vance was almost out of sight. I opened the door and double-timed it across the street trying to find the balance between a sprint and a jog. I charged between two houses and ended up on a parallel street. I caught a glimpse of Theresa just before she turned onto Crabapple Way, which I knew crossed Tall Oaks and connected to Long Field Drive and the entrance to her neighborhood.

I couldn't catch her from behind, so I ran between houses shadowing her route. Once she got to the entrance of the neighborhood she crossed Route 14 and headed for the King Kwik convenience store on the other side of the street. I crouched down behind the brick columns marking the entrance to her neighborhood and watched as she ran past the store entrance and jogged in place next to a pay phone. The phone must have rung, because she snatched the receiver and held it to her ear with two hands. I checked the time —9:00 on the dot.

The phone call explained her field trip to the convenience store. Nothing on her mobile or home phone records made me think she was talking to her son, but she could be using the pay phone to hide the calls.

But why the jogging? Why not drive there? She could be hiding the calls from her husband too. Daniel Schuster mentioned Thomas didn't visit Jacob at Pleasant Hill as often as his wife did, so it was likely Jacob had a tighter relationship with her. Tight enough to keep the lines of communication open after he went under. Maybe that was something Thomas didn't agree with and the jogging routine made for a more believable cover than Theresa taking evening drives.

Theresa only spoke for a few minutes then she hung up and jogged back the way she came. I dashed between the houses again, faster this time since I knew her route, and I was already in my SUV when she arrived at her home ten minutes later. She knew when that pay phone was going to ring. Did someone send her a message and tell her when to be there, or did she have a standing appointment at 9:00 p.m.? Only one way to find out.

I fired the ignition, left the neighborhood and pulled into the King Kwik parking lot. I slipped inside and poured a medium cup of coffee. Standing at the checkout counter I peered through the large front window, past the painted advertisements for lotto tickets and milk specials. The pay phone stood out of sight, which meant the clerk didn't see the call and probably couldn't tell me if a woman in a black jogging suit emblazoned in pink stripes was a common sight on certain evenings. I paid cash for the coffee, stepped outside and examined the pay phone. A blue-and-white sticker above the receiver read:

THIS TELEPHONE AND ALL ASSOCIATED EQUIPMENT IS THE property of South Land Communications. Anyone found defacing or tampering with this equipment will be subject to prosecution.

IF THIS TELEPHONE IS OUT OF SERVICE OR OTHERWISE DISABLED, please inform the clerk at this retail location.

LOCATION: 1053

. . .

THE NOTICE ALSO PROVIDED A TELEPHONE NUMBER AND ADDRESS for South Land Communications in Mobile, Alabama. I snapped a photo of the notice and climbed into my SUV. My gut told me Theresa and her son had arranged a schedule where he called this pay phone at a certain time on a certain day. Then again, my gut didn't always know its ass from an air freshener.

I would test my theory the next morning.

CHAPTER 12

PAY phones have been disappearing from the American landscape since the '90s. Now that everyone has a cell phone in their pocket there isn't much need for a quarter-munching dinosaur on every street corner or gas station parking lot.

Most of today's pay phones serve one of two purposes. They're either used to report a crime or commit one. Drug dealers and prostitutes love pay phones because they don't leave a paper trail. That was the same reason Theresa Vance used it. What Theresa and most criminals don't realize is that there is a paper trail. The call information for pay phone #1053 was tucked away safe and sound inside a computer at South Land Communications in Mobile, Alabama.

The major phone companies still own most of the country's pay phones, but thanks to deregulation smaller companies have snatched up a percentage of those units. I hoped South Land would cooperate with the friendly detective about to call their corporate offices.

I took a deep breath and dialed the number on the pay phone's sticker. After a few transfers Dave Reaves, the company's manager of southeast operations, picked up the line. I introduced myself as Roger Mathers, a detective with the Parkersburg Police Department.

"Our department has received several complaints from residents about dealers using one of your phones," I said. "Your unit 1053 seems to be a base of operations to distribute narcotics."

"That's unfortunate," said Reaves. "But I can't control who does what with our phones, detective."

"I understand that, but I've got a shitload of complaints here and I have to do something about it. There's enough information to open an investigation and that's why I'm calling. If I could establish a timeline for when calls are coming into that specific phone I might be able to find a pattern. Then I'd know when to put a man on the street to watch the phone."

"How do you want me to help?"

"If I had the call records for the phone—"

"You know I can't do without a—"

"Before you ask if I have a warrant, the answer is no," I said. "But I'm hoping we can take care of this without going that route, Dave."

"Why's that?"

"Because that's going to take more time than I have, and to be honest a judge won't sign off on the warrant anyway because I can't identify a specific dealer who's using your phone. Look, all I have to go on are thirty-some complaints about illegal activity at that location. I don't have the time or the manpower to stick someone on that corner to watch your phone until I identify a specific dealer, gather surveillance, get a warrant, call you back to get the call records, review those records, and so on. I'm asking for your cooperation so I can knock this out quickly and get back to all the other shit I don't have time for."

The story I blew up his ass was damn thin and I half expected him to tell me to fuck off.

"Plus, if you help us out it'll work in your favor," I said.

"How's that?"

"The neighborhood watch has organized an angry mob of

retirees who want to rip your phone out of the concrete. They're probably at home sharpening their pitchforks right now."

"That's vandalism and you can't—"

"Of course it is Dave, but that's how these things work. Neighborhoods see this as one of their only options. They figure if the phone goes away so will the illegal activity."

"They can't do that."

"Legally no. And I'm not an advocate for vigilante justice, but I can't stand next to your phone all day to ward them off."

"So what are you offering?"

"Send me the call records. I need incoming and outgoing calls for the past sixty days. You send me that and I should be able to identify a pattern, find my dealer and get 'em off the street quickly."

The other end was quiet.

"And you can guarantee no one is going to bust up our phone? Those aren't cheap to replace."

"I can't promise anything, but I can talk to the neighborhood watch group and tell them you're cooperating with us and that messing with your equipment isn't in their best interest. They just want these assholes out of their neighborhood. Got nothing against your equipment here."

It was weak, but I'd gotten more with less effort.

He was quiet again.

"All right. Just keep our company name out of it. We had a similar issue near Atlanta. Even had a boycott until we switched the phones there to outgoing calls only. I don't need that shit again."

"Help us out and you won't have any issues. And you won't have to replace the phone."

"Fine," he said. "Sixty days?"

"Right."

"You got a fax number?"

I gave him a number I used to receive faxes on my laptop and hoped he wouldn't call the Parkersburg Police Department to confirm the number or the story.

AN HOUR LATER REAVES SENT THE INFORMATION I NEEDED. I printed out the call log and scanned the sheet. The log showed a total of 327 calls placed from unit 1053 over the past two months, way more than I would have thought. I wasn't interested in outgoing calls though, I wanted to know how many calls came in. I circled the incoming calls on the printout and tallied twelve, all of which were placed from the same number, one with a Texas area code.

I scanned the rest of the log and identified the pattern. Whoever called Theresa dialed that pay phone's number every Sunday and Wednesday evening at nine o-clock. They only spoke for a few minutes, but they'd spoken every Sunday and Wednesday over the past two months. No exceptions. If I had a call report for the entire year, I suspected the pattern continued.

The idea that Jacob checked in with his mother for a few minutes twice a week fit the behavior profile of someone separated from his family who didn't want to cut ties completely.

I opened my laptop and accessed a reverse phone number database. A quick search revealed the calls originated from a commercial phone line registered at 1380 Cross Timbers Road in Flower Mound, Texas. Another pay phone.

Before I drove all the way to Texas I had to confirm whether Jacob Vance was on the other end of that pay phone. I had to wait until Wednesday to verify that. I closed the laptop and wondered how to kill two days in Parkersburg. I'd start with Kim Burton, Raymond Turner's girlfriend.

CHAPTER 13

KIM BURTON'S record at Pleasant Hill would be sealed so I had no idea what she did to get into the facility or how much time she spent there, but she'd be easy to find assuming she was still alive. Most criminals are repeat offenders, so I started with the clerk of courts database. If she had a record, I'd find hints of it there. I had to search through three counties before I found a record for a Kim Burton in Ritchie County, which was close enough to Parkersburg to pique my interest. Her age also fit.

According to record, Kim's landlord sued her for failure to pay rent. The case was closed shortly after it was filed, so she probably paid the obligation and moved on with her life. Even though the case was closed, the record gave me all the vital information I needed to find her.

Kim lived in Morgantown, West Virginia, about three hours east of Parkersburg. According to employment records she split her time cutting hair at a place called the Hair Loft and waitressing at an Olive Garden. I hoped she was at the restaurant, because if I left now I could make it to Morgantown by lunch.

. . .

I PULLED INTO THE RESTAURANT'S PARKING LOT A LITTLE AFTER noon. Since I had skipped breakfast, my stomach was making those sounds that send you to the kitchen. I stepped inside the lobby and asked the hostess to seat me in Kim's section. She probably thought I was a pathetic middle-aged man with a crush on the waitress, or one of Kim's relatives. Why else would I ask for a specific waitress at an Olive Garden?

"She's working the bar today, honey." The hostess pointed to the section behind her. "Just take a seat anywhere and she'll be right with you."

I walked into the bar area and grabbed a seat at a round table that was high enough to trigger vertigo. A few minutes later an attractive but tired-looking blond approached the table. She had long hair, pulled back into a tight ponytail. Several hair strands had come lose from the black elastic hair tie and hung lazily down the side of her face. That and the sweat stains on her white shirt told me she had been on her feet too long.

Her nametag read Kim B. and I didn't need her full last name to know who she was.

"Can I get you something to drink?"

I ordered an iced tea with no lemon. When she returned with that I ordered the pasta lunch special. She took the order on a notepad that she had tucked inside a fat black wallet. She slipped that into the front pocket of her apron. As she walked back toward the bar, I saw the unmistakable outline of a cell phone on the rear pocket of her tight black slacks.

The bar area was only half full and most of the patrons were probably local businesspeople breaking for lunch. I was a few sips into my iced tea when a younger couple walked in and sat at the table next to me. The guy wore a long-sleeved University of Delaware T-shirt and they looked like they were passing through town on their way someplace more exciting. After ordering their drinks the guy excused himself and walked to the bathroom. I set my glass on the table and followed him in.

"Excuse me," I said. "I was hoping you could help me out." He looked at me with raised eyebrows, probably wondering why I was talking to him in an Olive Garden bathroom.

"With what?" he said.

"Long story short, I'm a detective and I'm investigating your waitress."

"The lady at the bar?"

"That's right."

"What do you need my help with?"

"I won't go into a lot of detail, but when I finish my lunch I'm going to ask her a question that's going to piss her off. And then I'm going to leave. All I need you to do is watch her and let me know if she makes a phone call. That's it. You don't have to talk to her or anything."

"Just see if she makes a phone call?"

"Right." I slipped a fifty-dollar bill out of my wallet and handed it to him along with my business card. "Just do that and I'll buy your lunch."

"You just want me to tell you if she calls anyone and that's it?"

"Right. If she calls someone and you can tell me what she says, then I'll give you another fifty."

He thought for a moment, probably running through all the ways I could be full of shit.

"Okay."

"Thanks," I said and returned to my table.

My meal was on the table when I returned.

When I finished the pasta, Kim walked to the table and set the bill down in front of me. It was in the same type of wallet she kept her notepad in.

"I've got a strange question for you," I said.

"What's that?"

"I'm working on a book and I thought you might be able to help."

"A book? Not sure why you'd want to talk to me. Unless your book's about an overworked waitresses trying to raise two kids."

"No." I placed a hundred-dollar bill on top of the black wallet she'd plunked on the table and handed it back to her. "It's about Raymond Turner. I hear you know him."

She looked at the bill and then to me. "I don't have anything to say about him. Nothing at all. And I'd rather you not ask me anything else."

She clutched the wallet to her chest. "I'll be back with your change, sir."

"Keep it," I said.

"Your money ain't gonna make a difference. I still don't have anything to say about Ray."

"I know." I stood up and walked out of the bar, brushing past the man in the University of Delaware T-shirt on the way out.

There was a fine line between not *having* something to say about Turner and not *wanting* to say something about Turner. The twenty-something in the T-shirt would confirm which it was. If she was still close to Turner, her next step would be to call him. Maybe warn him or tip him off that someone was looking for him. If she made the call my next move would be to somehow lift her phone and search through the outbound history for a number. I could also get a look at her credit card statements and search for any airline or hotel purchases. If they still had some type of relationship after all these years maybe she traveled somewhere to see him.

I climbed into my Navigator and waited. A few minutes passed and my cell buzzed.

"She call anyone?" I said.

"No. I watched her for five minutes. She made two drinks and refilled the ice hopper behind the bar."

"That's it?"

"Yeah. That and I think she was crying because she reapplied some makeup. We'll probably be here for another twenty minutes. I'll let you know if she calls anyone, but so far nothing."

"Thanks for the help." I hung up the phone knowing she wouldn't dial Turner.

If someone you love is in hiding and someone like me comes looking for them, you make the call and tell them. You don't wait until the end of your shift, reapply your makeup, or refill the ice bin. You pull the phone from your back pocket and you dial. Kim Burton was a dead end and my investigation into Turner was off to a shitty start.

I arrived back in Parkersburg around four o'clock on Monday afternoon.

THE PAY PHONE WAS A STRONG LEAD AND I HOPED THAT BY Wednesday night, the next time Theresa slapped on her black and pink Spandex leggings and ran to that phone, I'd confirm whether she was talking to Jacob or someone else. I didn't have much to do until then, so I spent Monday evening strolling the streets of Parkersburg. I found a used bookstore and bought two Donald Westlake novels. I picked up *361* and *Somebody Owes Me Money* for $1.99 each and felt guilty about not paying more.

By Wednesday afternoon I had finished both books and took in a horror movie at the local cinema that charged four bucks per ticket, accepted only cash and sold soft drinks in the can.

CHAPTER 14

THERESA VANCE MIGHT HAVE INADVERTENTLY LED me to her son, but the only way I could confirm whether he was on the other side of that phone was to listen in on the conversation. I had a few pieces of information in my back pocket. Thanks to the telephone records from South Land I knew that phone would ring at 9 p.m. that evening, and I knew whoever was making the call was punching in the numbers from a pay phone in Flower Mound, Texas.

All signs pointed to Jacob on the other end, but I couldn't rule out an affair or some other person who might want to contact Theresa in secret. Identifying whom Theresa was talking to wouldn't be tough. It only took a roll of duct tape and an audio recorder. It would have been more difficult had the calling pattern been random, but Theresa and her secret caller traded unpredictability for convenience.

When I'd tailed Theresa three days ago she arrived at just the right time to answer that phone because she knew the exact time to be there. She'd probably used this routine for years, and I'd bet my two Westlake paperbacks she timed her route perfectly so she arrived at the phone seconds before that receiver rattled.

That night at 8:45 p.m. I drove passed the King Kwik convenience store and parked on the opposite corner of the street, a few hundred feet from the pay phone. I yanked my red Sony audio recorder from my coat pocket and clicked it on. Then I ripped a six-inch piece of duct tape from the gray roll and pressed it onto the back of the recorder being careful not to cover the tiny silver microphone. Placing the device in my hand, I opened the car door and stepped out. I crossed the street and had just stepped onto the cracked pavement of the King Kwik parking lot when a police cruiser pulled into the lot and parked. A uniformed officer and a teenage boy stepped out of the cruiser and stood talking next to the entrance.

Shit.

I tucked my hand closer to my side to hide the device. With the officer standing ten feet from the pay phone I couldn't risk placing the recorder, but if I didn't stash it soon I'd have to wait another four days, until next Sunday, to try again. I strolled past the officer and the teenager, gave them a nod and pushed open the heavy convenience store door. The door chime jingled above my head and the smell of hot dogs hit me. I didn't feel hungry, but now I wasn't sure. Once I made it to the back of the store, beyond the gaze of the large convex mirror mounted in the corner near the ceiling, I tucked the audio recorder into my waistband. I smoothed out the duct tape so the ends wouldn't stick to one another and buttoned my peacoat.

Except for the clerk behind the counter, I was the only person in the store. I wandered through the aisles trying to appear like I was looking for something. Every few feet I glanced up at the officer, waiting for him to either come in or leave, but he stood there chatting with his teenage friend.

My watch read 8:56 p.m. Theresa would arrive soon. I poured a small cup of nutty coffee from the lukewarm carafe next to the Krispy Kreme donut display and watched as the officer and the teenager talked in front of the store. The officer pointed down the street and the boy's head followed the motion. I slapped a dollar on the counter as the clerk set his magazine down and rang up the coffee. He swiped the dollar, stuffed it in the drawer and closed the register without saying anything. I nodded and walked toward the door.

From inside the store I saw Theresa jogging toward the entrance of her neighborhood. She was still a ways out, but the pink stripe bouncing up and down her leg gave her away. She was closing at a quick pace and would be at the phone in a few minutes.

I felt the clerk's eyes on me as I stared out the door. The officer turned and noticed me too. I opened the door and walked into the parking lot. I passed the officer and approached the pay phone. He said something to the boy about a high-speed pursuit through the area a few years ago. From the exchange I got the impression the kid was on a ride-along and the officer was doing his best to keep him interested. I approached the pay phone and set my coffee cup on top of the silver stand. In one smooth motion I removed the recorder from my waist, clicked the record button, and hastily stuck it to the underside of the pay phone stand with my right hand. At the same time I poked my left index finger into the coin return slot and flicked the swinging metal door, making sure the sound was loud enough for the officer to hear. I swiped my cup, turned back toward the officer and walked past him with my head down.

"Old habit," I said. "If I see a pay phone I have to check for change. Never find shit these days."

He cracked a smile and I crossed the street just as Theresa jogged behind me. A moment later the phone rang, but was quickly silenced as Theresa jerked the receiver from the cradle. I didn't turn around, but I imagined the officer and the kid wondered why she was taking a call in a convenience store parking lot. There wasn't anything illegal about it, and Theresa Vance looked as much like a criminal as the kid in the button-up dress shirt and khakis standing next to the police officer.

I slipped into my Navigator and watched as Theresa swayed

back and forth in front of the phone. I knew the conversation wouldn't last long—never more than three or four minutes according to the call log. Just enough time for Theresa and her caller to share a few thoughts and be on their way. Part of me felt bad for Theresa. As a parent myself, I tried to think about what it would be like to hear about your kid's life through a few three-minute phone calls every week. But every time I found myself feeling sorry for her I thought about those crime scene photos and what happened to Josh Baker and Theresa's problems faded away like the sun burning off an early morning fog.

After a few minutes Theresa hung up the phone, looked over her shoulder and jogged out of the parking lot. As she crossed the street the cruiser pulled out of the lot and sped down the street toward something more exciting.

I waited until Theresa passed through the entrance to her neighborhood before I climbed out of the car, walked across the parking lot, snatched my recorder from the underside of the phone stand and stopped the recording. I wanted to play back the recording right there in the lot, but I waited until I returned to the car.

My thumb trembled as I held it above the play button. I took a long drink from my Styrofoam coffee cup and clicked on the unit. Theresa's voice was the first one I heard.

"Hello," she said.

"Hi again," said the man on the other end, his faint voice crackling. It sounded like an old drive-in movie speaker, the dull metal kind Albert used to clip to our station wagon window when I was a kid.

The exchange was brief. Over the course of three minutes the male voice shared snippets of the past few days with Theresa. His voice cut in and out, which I expected considering my sophisticated approach of taping a digital recorder to the underside of a pay phone. For as old as it was, the recorder had a sensitive mic and while I didn't expect to get the entire exchange, I hoped I could get what I needed.

The man talked about some childcare business and said they were adding a few more children to the roster. He said something about an X-ray revealing he might need surgery, but I couldn't make out the details. He asked Theresa if she was looking forward to Thanksgiving and she replied she was. He didn't say anything to identify himself until the final seconds of the call.

"Tell Dad I said hello," he said. For some reason, that part of the conversation came through as if he were standing right next to me.

"You know I can't do that," said Theresa. She laughed nervously and I got the feeling every call ended the same way.

They exchanged goodbyes and Theresa hung up.

I clicked off the audio recorder and tossed it into the cup holder on my console.

Theresa and Thomas Vance only had one son. I had my guy.

Time to go to Texas and find Jacob Vance.

CHAPTER 15

THAT NIGHT I slept in my own bed in Cincinnati. The person I hoped was Jacob Vance wasn't going to call Theresa again until Sunday evening. It would take two days to drive to Flower Mound, Texas, to sit on that pay phone, which meant I could spend Thursday and Friday at home before a two-day drive put me in Texas on Sunday afternoon.

I arrived at my apartment a little before one o'clock in the morning. Albert was already asleep when I dropped my suitcase in my room and hit the pillow harder than I had in a long time.

That night I dreamt of Josh Baker. In the dream, I stood in a lush green field that looked like it should be inside a lawn care company's brochure. Josh stood in front of me. He stood inside a patch of dead brown grass, a perfect circle maybe two-feet in diameter. It took me a moment to realize it was Josh. I'd never seen a clear photo of him. All of the images I had seen in the newspaper coverage were black-and-white photos, each one grainier than the last. The crime scene photos only showed the left side of Josh's face, which was obscured by blood. The etching of his face on his gravestone lacked any detail, so the dream was the first time I got to take him all in.

He didn't say anything, only stared at me with a look that I guessed was pity.

A tall man stood next to Josh holding his hand. I tried to focus on his face to make out the detail, but I couldn't. I looked straight at him but I couldn't describe a single feature on his face. The only thing that stood out about him was the ground beneath his feet. Unlike Josh's brown patch, this man stood in the same lush green grass as the field in front of me. I stared at the man, but the more I tried to look at him the harder it became to focus. His face was like a floater in your eye—the moment you try to find it, it darts to the side. I waited for Josh to say something but he didn't. He only stared at me. After a moment the man placed his palm flat on the top of Josh's head, as if indicating that our brief time together was over, and I woke up.

I walked in on Albert making eggs in the kitchen around nine o'clock in the morning. He hadn't heard me come into the apartment, and by the way he jumped back and grabbed a kitchen knife I knew I had startled him.

"Jesus Christ, son."

"Did I scare you?"

"Not you exactly. Just your beard." He turned back to his sizzling skillet. "It's like a face fungus or something."

I ran my hands down the side of my face. I did need a trim. Not a shave, but a trim.

"You know what would look good with that beard?" he said.

"What's that?"

"A red flannel shirt and a sharp axe."

I laughed and poured a cup of coffee.

"When you get back in?"

"Late last night."

"Still in West Virginia?"

"I was. I need to be in Texas by Sunday night."

"What's in Texas?"

"One of the guys I'm looking for."

"One of? How many people are on your list?"

"Just two," I said.

"How long you going to be there?"

"Not sure, but hoping not long."

Albert scooped his eggs out of the skillet and slid them onto a piece of toast. He pointed to the range. "You want me to leave this on?"

"That depends. We out of eggs?"

"Yes," he said.

"Then no."

I followed him to the table and sat down with my coffee. "How's Brooke and Becca?"

"Good. She's dropping Becca off tomorrow night. We're going to do Dewey's for pizza." He took a bite and pointed his egg sandwich at me. "You said you have to be in Texas on Sunday, so that means you're here for a few days."

"I'll leave first thing Saturday morning."

"Good, then you can come with us. Brooke was going to join us. Hope that's okay."

"I don't have a problem with it."

He wiped his chin with his hand. "So what's going on with you two? Am I going to need to find a new place to live?"

"Why would you need to do that?"

"Figured if you two got back together you wouldn't need your old man helping around the house."

"First off, you don't help around the house. You eat all the eggs and make weak coffee. And second, why am I the only one who isn't part of this getting-back-together conversation? We haven't really talked about it."

"She mentioned it to me the other day. Asked what I thought about it."

"What do you think about it?"

He shrugged and shoved a bite into his mouth. "Don't much matter. Course it would be good for Becca. She'd get to live with her parents again."

"I don't know if that's a good thing or not. The last thing I want to do is put her in a position to see the cracks form again. Sometimes it's better to have a strong splintered family than weak whole one." I sipped my coffee. "Guess we'll cross that bridge when we come to it."

THE NEXT NIGHT WE FOUND OUR USUAL TABLE AT DEWEY'S PIZZA and burned the roofs of our mouths on the best pizza in Cincinnati. Becca and I have had dinner there every Friday night since Brooke and I split five years ago. Albert joined us once we moved in together. Consistency didn't show its face much in my line of work, but Becca's weekend sleepovers and dinner at Dewey's on Friday night were anchors in an otherwise tumultuous sea. I already felt like garbage having to miss out on Becca's sleepovers until I wrapped the Baker case, and if I had a chance to make our standing Friday night tradition I was damn sure going to take it.

Brooke joining us was different. Albert had suggested it, and given Brooke's recent breakup with Dr. Dickhead, I figured she could use the company. Brooke and I exchanged casual conversation and awkward glances throughout the meal. Albert must have sensed Brooke wanted a minute alone with me, because as soon as the waitress exchanged the aluminum pizza tray for the bill he suggested he and Becca visit the patio to watch the koi in the pond.

"Did you think about what I said the other day?" asked Brooke. "About spending more time together?"

"Hard not to think about it, but I get the feeling this is some knee-jerk reaction to you leaving Daryl. Not much has changed in my life and all the reasons you left me and ran for the hills are still in play."

"I did lay it on pretty hard didn't I? About your job and not knowing if you'd come home at night."

"I seem to remember something about me getting shot and bleeding to death in an alley." I patted my chest searching for bullet holes. "So far, I've only got holes where they're supposed to be."

She laughed. "Let's hope that streak continues." She reached for the check but I grabbed it out from under her fingers.

"What is it that you're looking for Brooke? What's going to make this time different?"

"I don't know. I've had a lot of time to think about the decision I made and I'm not sure it was the right one."

"I can't shake the feeling it's all going to come crumbling down again."

"So what if it does? What's the worst that could happen?"

"Oh, I don't know, maybe we break a little girl's heart again. That's enough to make me weary."

She nodded. "Then maybe we ease into it. See if it works. That's all I'm asking."

I slipped three $20s inside the black wallet with the bill. "I don't plan on changing my line of work. This is what I do and I'm happy doing it."

"You still plan on hanging out with shady people who like to shoot at one another?"

"It probably sounds corny and stupid to you, but I like the feeling of helping people who can't help themselves."

"Corny, yes, stupid, no. Look, you don't have to sell me on it. I know you wouldn't be doing this…" She waved her hands in the air. "Whatever this is if it didn't mean something to you. I guess I'd rather live with you and your job than not be in your life."

"I have to go to Texas tomorrow morning and might be gone for a while. It'll give me some time to think about everything. Let's chat about it when I get back."

"Sounds good to me. I'm not going anywhere."

The waitress collected the cash and I told her to keep the change. Albert materialized a moment later with Becca, who wore a wide smile.

"Why is it you always disappear when the check comes?" I said.

"Just a coincidence."

Becca clinched her teeth together like she was trying to hold back a secret that was trying to get out. "Papaw fed the fish some M&Ms. They swallowed them whole."

Albert gently elbowed her in the side, as if she had spoiled the twist ending to a movie.

"I don't think fish are supposed to eat M&Ms," I said.

Albert shrugged. "They fell out of my pocket."

Becca giggled.

"Right. Well, I think it's time to wrap this up."

We retuned to my apartment and spent the night playing board games and watching a Disney movie. At one point I turned to see Albert, Brooke and Becca laughing at the television. We almost looked like a family again, something I hadn't seen in a long time. After the movie I tucked Becca into bed and walked Brooke to the door. She kissed me, then walked down the breezeway clutching her coat tight around her.

I climbed into bed and closed my eyes and thought about my trip to Texas in the morning.

CHAPTER 16

On Saturday I left Cincinnati before Becca and Albert woke up and drove until I crossed the Arkansas boarder, where I grabbed a hotel room for the night. On Sunday, I arrived in Flower Mound, Texas, around two in the afternoon.

According to the pay phone record from South Land and the results from the reverse phone search, the calls to the King Kwik parking lot originated from a pay phone at a grocery store near the corner of Shiloh Road and Cross Timbers Road in Flower Mound.

I checked into a Travelodge five miles from the pay phone. I assumed Vance lived somewhere in the area, as I didn't think he'd intentionally drive out of his way twice a week to make a phone call, especially if he didn't think someone was watching him. I wasted a few hours in my hotel room before grabbing my binoculars and returning to my car.

I arrived at the grocery store at seven o'clock and found the pay phone at the corner of the parking lot. I compared the telephone number from the South Land report to the label on the phone. It matched. I felt my pulse jump at the thought of Jacob Vance picking up that receiver in the next two hours.

There was a buffet restaurant across the street from the grocery store, a good location to wait until Vance arrived. After getting a bite to eat, I returned to my car and waited. Jacob Vance, or at least the person I assumed was Jacob Vance, was as punctual as his mother. At 8:55 p.m. a dark blue Toyota SUV pulled into the grocery store lot and parked a few spaces from the phone. I yanked my binoculars from the console and watched for whoever was in the car to approach the pay phone.

A few minutes later the SUV backed out of its parking spot and rolled next to the phone so the driver could make the call without getting out of the vehicle.

Damn. No visual.

I peered through the binoculars and jotted the SUV's license plate number on my pad. When I got back to my hotel I could run the license plate through the DMV database and get Jacob Vance's new name. I'd use that name to build a new profile, and if my gut was right I would find a slew of information that began in 1992, the year Jacob Vance vanished.

I was eyeballing the Toyota through the binoculars when three tractor-trailers blew by blocking my line of sight. I wiped the sweat from my brow and peered back through the lenses only to see the SUV pulling away from the phone and onto Cross Timbers Road. I tossed the binoculars onto the passenger seat and fired up my engine as the SUV passed in front of me. A moment later I was on the road, about ten cars behind it.

The Toyota traveled east and I was able to hang far enough behind it to blend in with the other traffic. It took a left onto Long Prairie Road and the two cars directly behind it followed. I made the turn as well and was now only a few cars back. Had it been daylight, I would have been more concerned about Vance burning me in his rearview mirror. Tailing someone requires a complicated dance to avoid being made, but most of those steps go out the window when night falls.

About two miles later he veered onto Dixon Lane. I turned

behind him and eased off the accelerator to give him some distance. That's when a gray Ford Explorer slammed into the front passenger side of my Navigator knocking my messenger bag and most of Willie's files into my lap and sending my two-and-a-half-ton SUV into the median. After plowing me into a guardrail, the Ford spun 90 degrees and came to a stop in front of me. The Explorer nailed me hard and I couldn't shake the feeling this was an omen that I shouldn't be looking for Vance.

I wasn't sure if my head actually hit the driver's window, but it felt like it. I wiped my hand across my forehead expecting to find blood, but it was clear. I took a moment to clear the cobwebs from my noggin, clean up the files that littered the floor in front of me, and reached for the door handle. When I stepped out of the vehicle a slender black woman was standing in front of me.

She had long wavy black hair that reached the middle of her back and she wore red-framed eyeglasses that looked expensive. She was dressed like she wanted to be noticed but not leered at. She looked important.

"Are you okay?" she asked as I rubbed my head.

"Yeah, I'm fine. You?"

"Yes. I'm so sorry." She pointed to the side street across from us. "I was trying to pull out of there and I didn't see you. I'm so sorry. Are you sure you're okay?"

"I'm fine." I looked past the woman, up the road, and thought I saw Vance's Toyota disappearing over a hill.

"We should probably exchange insurance information," she said.

I walked around my Navigator and looked at the gaping hole, the size of a beagle, next to my passenger front tire. I snapped off a jagged piece of fender that clung to the wheel well and tossed it inside my car.

"I'm sorry about your car," she said. "I've never been in an accident before." She grabbed an oversized tan purse from her vehicle, opened it on the hood of the Ford and found her wallet.

She glanced at the damage to the front of her car and then at mine.

"Here's my insurance information," she said, handing me a red-and-white card. I scanned the card. Her name was Valerie Cheatham.

For the past decade, whenever I needed an alias I always used the name Roger Mathers. There's a reason for that. Roger Mathers was born three days after I was born. We both came into this world at Bethesda North Hospital and were similar in height and weight. Unfortunately for Roger he died in an auto accident two decades ago, something that seemed ironic as I stared at my wounded SUV. I didn't think Roger would mind that I had used his birth certificate, social security number, and a variety of other vital records as my cover. I had a full array of identification badges with his name and my photo on them. One thing I did not have was an insurance card.

"Why don't we just forget about it?" I said, moving my hand like blackjack player waving off a hit. "You can take care of your damage and I'll take care of mine. It'll work out in your favor, anyway. No need to get the insurance companies involved."

"I really think we should exchange information. My husband'll kill me if I show up with my car looking like this and no insurance info."

I pulled Roger Mathers's driver's license from my wallet. The gust from a passing pickup truck nearly blew it out of my hand. "Here's my ID. I'm a private investigator and the vehicle is registered to my agency." I handed her a business card. "I don't have an insurance card, but if you contact me at this number, I'll get you the information when I'm back in Ohio."

She took the card from my hand and shot me a suspicious look. "You don't have insurance do you?"

"I do have insurance, but this is a company vehicle and I don't have a card for it." I snapped a photo of her insurance card with my phone and handed it back to her. She grabbed a pen from her purse and jotted down my license information on the back of the business card.

"Okay, but I'm writing down your license plate too." She handed back my license. "In case I need it later."

"My front plate is probably stuck in your bumper somewhere. Just take it with you." I smiled. She didn't.

Ten minutes after first burying her grill into the side of my Navigator Valerie pulled back onto the street and drove off, leaving me with a headache and a few grand in bodywork. I got back into my vehicle and fired up the engine. While I wasn't able to tail Vance to wherever he went, I had his license plate number and could still locate him through the DMV.

I eased back onto Dixon Lane hoping my Navigator could hold a straight line and limped back to the Travelodge. My car pulled to the right more than usual, but it was still drivable. Besides the occasional piece of debris that fell off the front of the car and the annoying whistling as air rushed through the fractures in my fender, it drove pretty well. It was slower than normal on account it was now as aerodynamic as a washing machine wearing a top hat, but I hadn't planned any high-speed pursuits. I only needed it to survive long enough to find Vance and get back to Cincinnati.

When I got back to the hotel I grabbed my laptop and my printer from the back of my car and hoped they still worked after getting bounced across the back seat. Halfway between my Navigator and my hotel room I got dizzy. Somehow I found my balance and made it to my room. Once inside I laid down on the bed to rest my head. It throbbed enough to take my concentration away from Jacob Vance. I closed my eyes, content to pick back up on Vance in the morning. As I felt sleep overtaking me I wondered if I would dream about Josh Baker again.

CHAPTER 17

MONDAY MORNING I woke up with a slight headache, but nothing like the night before. After getting a coffee and a banana nut muffin from the Travelodge cafe I returned to my room to dig deeper into Jacob Vance.

It didn't take me long to find what I thought was Vance's new identity. His license plate was registered to Jake Polling, who lived here in town. I thought back to what Gypsy Scott said about people in WITSEC keeping their first names to avoid confusion. It wasn't the only confirmation I needed to tie Jake Polling to Jacob Vance, but it was a start, and a damn good one.

Jake Polling's driver's registration provided everything I needed to get started. His birthdate was June 7, 1975, which according to the booking record in Willie's case file was exactly one month later than Jacob Vance's birthdate. Gypsy Scott didn't mention anything about birthdates, but it seemed logical the Feds would assign Vance a new birthday that was easy to remember, and a month off from his real date seemed like it fit.

I also had Jake Polling's social security number. I ran a trace using his digits and found the social security number was assigned the same month Vance was released from Pleasant Hill. The stars lined up too straight to be a coincidence.

I ran Polling's information through the criminal record database expecting to find something. I was convinced someone like him couldn't walk on the right side of the law forever. After doing what he did to Josh Baker, I'd bet Albert's retirement savings that Vance had reoffended. But according to the criminal record search he was clean.

A search through his employment records showed Jake Polling owned and operated Tot Spot Child Care Center in Flower Mound. That's when I had him. Anyone who operated a childcare center had to be licensed by the state. That license required successfully passing a detailed background check, which meant his fingerprints were on file with the state.

There are a variety of traits you can change to become someone else. You can alter your appearance, location, habits, mannerisms, style of dress and speech patterns. You can't change your DNA or your fingerprints. And while I didn't have Vance's DNA to test, I did have the next best thing—his inky fingers.

I reached for Willie's gray bag, dumped it onto the bed and rummaged through the pile of papers until I found Vance's booking card, complete with his then nine-year-old fingerprints. An interesting fact about fingerprints is they don't change. They grow right along with you, and any unique markings on your thumb at four years old will be there at forty-four years old.

If I could get a copy of Jake Polling's childcare license background check, I could compare his fingerprints with Jacob Vance's prints. I was pretty sure I had the right guy, now I had to confirm it.

A quick Internet search revealed that Texas, like many other states, had a childcare license program. It's a central database accessible through the Texas State Department of Early Learning, which was maintained by the Texas Department of Public Safety. The central database served two purposes. On the public-facing side, it offered peace of mind by allowing parents seeking a responsible childcare facility to search local providers and confirm whether they had a license to operate. The database also served a more utilitarian purpose for providers by allowing them to initiate and manage employee background checks. As childcare providers hired new staff they scheduled background checks and fingerprint scans with the state. New employees had to pass this check before they could have direct contact with children. An administrator from the childcare center could log into the database to monitor the background check progress, download forms and print out certificates. I knew from a previous case these types of databases also stored fingerprint images for download. Unfortunately, that information was restricted only to those with administrative access. I scanned the website and clicked on the childcare provider log-in page. It asked for an email address and password, neither of which I had.

If you're using a simple password, a hacker can crack it in a few seconds using an automated program. The more complicated the password, the longer it takes. If you're using a long password with a combination of numbers, letters and symbols it can take years for these programs to break it. That's why most websites require a fascinating array of characters before it approves a password.

In addition to the overwhelming odds of cracking a sophisticated password, I had no idea how to do it. I wasn't a hacker, and while I knew several hackers who had helped me out in the past, the idea that someone can simply slip into a network and access anything they want is part urban legend and part Hollywood hype.

Luckily, cracking into a secure website is less about finding a backdoor in the code and more about asking permission. You just have to be creative in the way you ask.

I created an email address for a fictional Beth Collins and set it to forward to my encrypted email account. Then I found the technical support number for the Texas Department of Public Safety and dialed. After sitting on hold for ten minutes, I was connected to a tech named Jason, who actually sounded like a genuine Texan and not some outsourced IT tech from overseas. I could hear the cowboy hat through the phone.

"Jason, this is Jake Polling," I said as I cranked up the volume of my hotel television for background noise, "from Tot Spot here in Flower Mound and I need to add an admin to my account."

"Thanks for calling, Mr. Polling. I can assist you with that. You can add a user from the main menu under accounts—"

"That's the problem," I interrupted. "I'm sitting at a terminal in DFW, and while I have my laptop with me I didn't pack my power cord. I'm dead in the water."

"If you can call me back when you're in the office I can walk you through the process."

"That's just it," I said. "I'm boarding a flight to Italy in a half hour and I'll be gone for three weeks. I had planned to log in and add her before I boarded, but that's when my computer died. We're hiring two new employees and I need one of my assistants to log into the system to run the background checks. I can't wait until I get back and I don't know what kind of access I'll have once I land. Isn't there anything you can do to help me?"

"Can you log into the system on a smartphone?"

"Not with these eyes. I'm blind as a bat when it comes to small screens. Can't see a damn thing. Have to use the voice options for most everything. I'd give her my log in information but I can't remember it. We used to have someone at the office who managed all this, so I never logged in myself, but she left and I've got no idea what my username or password is."

"I'm afraid that's not information I can give out over the phone."

"I wouldn't ask you to do that, but can you add a new admin for me? If you can add her to the system, I can have her log in with her own information."

Jason was silent for a moment. He probably ran through all the possible solutions in his head. The great thing about speaking with tech support is that they are trained to help people. It's their job to find solutions, and I could use that expectation to get into the system. They're also trained to not give out passwords or personal information, but I wasn't asking for that.

"So you want to add an admin?"

"Right. Beth is going to manage the system going forward anyway, so if you could set her up that would be great."

"What's her name?"

"Beth Collins."

He stopped. “Before we go any further, can you confirm your date of birth and you social security number, Mr. Polling?"

"Sure." I glanced at the workup I'd compiled on Polling and rattled off the information.

"Okay," said Jason. "What's Beth's email address?"

"It's BethCollins@totspottexas.com."

"Okay. One moment." Jason slapped several keys on his keyboard. "Okay, I registered her with the system, but she is going to have to go in and complete her profile."

"Great. So she'll have access to upload and maintain any records, since she'll be handling that from now on?"

"Right. The first time she logs in she'll use the default password. That's gonna be password123%, but it'll prompt her to change it as soon as she logs in for the first time."

"Perfect. I'll let her know. Thanks for the help, Jason."

"Sure. Is there anything else I can help you with?"

"That'll do it. You just made my trip a lot less stressful."

I clicked off my phone and headed downstairs to the cafe for a coffee refill and to give the database enough time for Beth Collins's information to update. When I returned to my room I accessed the Texas Department of Public Safety's website, clicked to the Texas State Department of Early Learning link and logged in using Beth Collins's phantom email address and the temporary password Jason assigned. A menu gave me two options, "Submit a new employee for background review" or "Manage existing employees." I clicked on the manage employees tab and saw a list of about a dozen individuals who worked at Tot Spot, including Jake Polling. I clicked on Polling's name and his profile page opened on my screen. There, at the top of the page, was a "Fingerprints" tab. I clicked that and watched as ten postage-stamp sized boxes, each with a clear fingerprint scan, loaded in front of me.

Gotcha. I clicked "print" and waited as my inkjet hummed.

Television crime shows make fingerprint analysis out to be some otherworldly science. If you're trying to identify someone from a latent print then a lot hinges on the process. If an investigator doesn't lift a print correctly, or if the sample gets damaged or deteriorates, it can be tough to make a clear comparison. Movies love to show the scene where a detective has two prints on the computer screen and they merge together into one as he gets a hit on the AFIS database and confirms they've got their guy. That makes for great entertainment, and it might be an accurate portrayal of how to find a match for a latent print, but comparing two prints to confirm whether they're identical isn't nearly as exciting or as difficult. No computer needed.

Comparing prints for a match to a known sample requires a few items. It takes two sets of prints, a magnifying glass and knowing what to look for. At first glance a fingerprint can be intimidating with all the waves, ridges and hypnotic patterns. But a fingerprint is much like a Las Vegas craps table—it's only as intimidating as you make it. Focus on the specific things you need to look for and comparing fingerprints is as easy as finding the red flag on a mailbox.

I had my two prints, but unlike Sherlock Holmes I didn't carry a magnifying glass in my overcoat. If I was lucky, the stocked minibar had the next best thing. Inside the refrigerator, next to the small vials of rum and vodka and the seven-dollar bottle of water, was a 20-ounce plastic bottle of Coke. I dumped out the Coke into the bathroom sink and used a small pocketknife on my key ring to cut a circular piece the size of a half dollar from the bottle's curved neck.

I tuned on the desk light and placed Vance's 1984 booking card next to the printout of Polling's fingerprints. I focused on the right index finger because it looked like the cleanest image on both samples.

Comparing prints comes down to focusing on the areas where patterns converge into each other, where ridges start and stop, and where ridges split into two. By marking five or six of these unique elements, you can compare the second print to confirm if these elements are in the same place as they are in the control print. If they are, then the prints are a match.

It's like comparing two dot-to-dot pictures. You don't have to look at the completed drawing with the lines connecting the dots to confirm a match. You don't need the lines at all. If you can confirm the dots are in the same place on each sheet you've got a match.

I got lucky because these were both clean prints. Sometimes prints lifted from crime scenes can be smudged or partial or otherwise poor samples to work with, but the booking prints were taken at the police station by a professional and the Polling prints were taken by a fingerprint scan at some government office. Time to get to work.

I held the concave plastic piece I'd cut from the Coke bottle over the booking card and examined the right index finger print through my makeshift magnifying glass. I started at the core of the print and counted to the left four ridges, where I found the first split in a ridge. I marked the spot with the hotel pen they left in the desk drawer and continued examining the print. Two ridges to the left of the first split was a point where a ridge ended. A new ridge began just above it. I marked that spot as well. I moved another three ridges to the left and found a point where the ridge split twice. I marked both splits and looked for any additional nearby anomalies. Just below the last point I marked were two specks. These were areas where the ridges were so short that instead of resembling a line they looked like dots. I marked both those points and swapped Jacob Vance's booking card for Jake Polling's printout.

I squinted, bent back over the desk and examined the printout looking at the specific locations I'd marked on the booking print. Each anomaly matched. The ridge stops and starts, the splits and the dots were all in the same place on Polling's print. I had my guy.

Now it was time to meet him in person.

CHAPTER 18

I DO MOST of my work from a distance. I rarely find myself face-to-face with the people I'm paid to locate. Don't need to. It's safer looking for someone from a comfortable couch or coffee shop. Most of the time I only need to get someone's name and location and then I pass that on to whoever is paying the bill. Then I'm out. Impersonal is how I like it. This wasn't one of those times.

All the evidence I'd gathered told me Jacob Vance was Jake Polling, but since giving Willie Baker his identity would sign his death warrant I wanted the chance to look him in the eye. To look into his soul. There was a curiosity component to it too. Part of me wanted to meet this monster in person and see what he was like. It's not often I get the chance to come face-to-face with pure evil, and I wasn't going to let the opportunity slip past.

Tot Spot was about ten miles away from my hotel, so I grabbed my bag and my .45 and headed for the lobby. I passed the front desk, where two couples stood at the counter checking in, and walked through the revolving glass door. I had momentarily forgotten about yesterday's car accident, but the sight of my crumpled fender brought it all back. I didn't look forward to Albert's comments about me not being able to drive for shit or his sly comparisons to Columbo's jalopy. I climbed in the car, started the engine and pulled out onto the main road. I made several turns on my way to see Vance and noticed the silver SUV behind me made the same turns. That made me nervous.

Gypsy Scott warned me that I might draw unwanted attention once I started shaking bushes, and the silver SUV caught my interest. There are a few easy ways to confirm if you're being tailed. The first is to make two right turns. If someone is still on your ass after that, you've got a reason to be suspicious. I made the two rights and the SUV still pursued, but it dropped back, the same way I did when I followed Vance after he left the pay phone. I didn't like it. There was an intersection up ahead and I slowed and clicked my right turn signal on. The SUV in the rearview mirror did the same. As soon as I saw his signal I turned mine off and sped through the intersection. He turned off his signal and followed. He was burned and he knew it. I slowed again and this time made a U-turn in the median and headed back toward the hotel. He didn't follow. He probably thought I'd made him and he wanted to drop the tail and pick me up again later. He already knew to find me at the Travelodge, so I figured I'd see him again.

A moment later it wasn't the silver SUV that concerned me, it was the blue Fusion that stayed on me after another two turns. Sophisticated surveillance requires multiple vehicles to tail a mark. One vehicle drops off and another picks up. They keep this up so the mark can't pinpoint a specific vehicle behind him. I figured the silver SUV dropped off after I made him and the Fusion took over. Time to find out who had such an interest in me.

A mile later it was still on me. I slowed and parked on the street in front of the Rise and Grind coffee shop. The Fusion parked on the opposite side of the street but stayed a hundred feet behind me. Whatever game we were playing was about to get more interesting. I slipped the .45 from my leather messenger bag, placed it in my lap and then realigned my side mirror so I could watch the car. I could make out a woman in the driver's seat. Unless there was someone tucked away on the floor in the backseat, she was the only one in the vehicle.

I waited for a few minutes half expecting her to approach my car, but she didn't. After five minutes it was obvious she was staying inside her vehicle. Time to take it to the next level. I stashed the .45 under my seat, stepped out of the car and went inside the coffee shop. I ordered a large black coffee and a banana nut muffin from the hipster in the flannel shirt behind the counter and took a seat at a table in the corner of the cafe. There was a stainless steel napkin dispenser on the table, the kind you find in old diners. When I adjusted it to the right angle I could clearly see the Fusion across the street, but whoever was in the car couldn't see me. It wasn't as clear as my car mirror, but it did the trick.

In all the years I've been tracking people down, I've learned that the best strategy to finding someone is to make them find you. That strategy hadn't worked for Vance, and I was still thinking about how to apply it to Turner, but I'd focus on him later. I was more concerned about the woman in the Fusion, and I figured if I sat in the cafe long enough she would become suspicious and sweat the fact I hadn't come out. I hoped she would assume that I made her and ditched her in the cafe by slipping out a back door. Had I wanted to lose her, that's exactly what I would have done. I would have slipped out the back, rounded the corner and waited for her to cross the street and enter the cafe to confirm whether I was still there. Then I'd jump into my car and lose her before she had a chance to make it back to her vehicle.

But I didn't want to lose her. I wanted to identify her and see what part she played in this little game. I sipped my coffee and waited. For the next hour I watched the hazy reflection on the napkin dispenser. Then I saw it. Her curiosity got to her and she wanted to see if I was still inside. She stepped out of the car, crossed the street and walked into the cafe.

She jostled a large tan purse in her hand, scanned the room and saw me sitting in the corner. I shot her a wide smile and watched as she ordered a coffee and then sat at a table against the opposite wall. I imagined she felt part relieved she hadn't lost me, and part embarrassed she let herself get drawn into the trap I'd set.

She crossed her arms in front of her and stared at the steam rising from the white ceramic mug. She stirred the coffee with a narrow straw without putting anything in it and then glared at me. It took me a moment to realize where I'd seen her before. He hair was pulled back in a tight ponytail and that's what threw me. Had it been down, I would have recognized her from the first time we met. When she plowed her Ford Explorer into the side of my Navigator. That was one hell of a coincidence, which was bad because I didn't believe in coincidences.

I walked past her to get a refill at the counter and then slipped into the seat across from her on my way back.

"Hi," I said, eyeing her full mug.

"Hello."

"This isn't much of a place for someone who doesn't drink coffee."

"I assume it's not."

"So you want to tell me why you're following me? I'd rather talk about it than risk any more bodywork to my car. Another collision and my insurance company might drop me. It was a good way to get my identification though. Nice work."

"Thanks. But you gave me an alias. You're not Roger Mathers."

"Says who?"

She pulled a file from her purse and slapped it onto the table with a thud. "Says the FBI."

I sipped my dark roast and leaned back in my seat. "Whatcha got there?"

"I ran your name through our database and found a report filed by Special Agent Brian Tipton two years ago. The Roger Mathers name came back as a known alias of Finn Harding, ex-private investigator. Got your photo from your PI license to confirm it. Your suspended license."

"So you're FBI?"

"No. I'm with the US Marshals Service. Deputy Marshal Valerie Cheatham." She didn't extend her hand.

"Good to see you again. Is Uncle Sam going to pay for the hole in my car? Figure you're liable given you hit me in the line of duty."

"I'll look for the hitting-a-suspect's-car-during-an-investigation form when I'm back in the office."

"Suspect?" I took another sip. "As far as I know there's no reason why I should be a suspect for anything. So why the tail?"

"Because I want to know why you're looking for him."

"Who?"

She smirked, knowing I tried to get her to acknowledge Vance's new identity. "Why are you looking for Jacob Vance?"

"I'm not looking for him," I said. "I found him."

"Maybe you did and maybe you didn't."

"If I hadn't found him we wouldn't be having this conversation. And my car would look a lot better than it does."

"Suppose you had found him. Why were you looking for him in the first place?"

"I'm working on a case—"

"Ex PIs don't work cases."

I drew in a deep breath. "I'm just looking into him for a friend."

"Some journalist hire you? Someone related to the victim maybe?"

"The victim? You mean Josh Baker. You can use his name."

"I'm familiar with the case, and now I want to be familiar with why you're in Texas."

"I'm working with an author. She hired me to dig up some information on Vance and Turner. That's not illegal."

"No, it's not, but there's a gag order on the case."

I smirked at her attempt to scare me away. "That doesn't apply to me. Only to anyone involved with the original case, which I wasn't. And neither was the author, so she can write whatever she wants with no blowback."

"That might be true, but if your author friend publishes anything that shouldn't be out there, the court can haul her in and demand she reveal her source. You might not be under the order, but my guess is that someone who is feeding you information is. The gag order could apply to them and that threat alone could make a publisher nervous. My guess is she never lands a book deal."

"Then you've got nothing to worry about."

She tapped her red nails on the tabletop. "My gut tells me otherwise."

I smiled. "That could just be an internal injury from T-boning my car."

She didn't say anything.

"I assume you're hiding Raymond Turner too?"

"I don't know anything about that."

"Bullshit," I said. "You can't play dumb now. I already know you're protecting Vance so you're probably protecting Turner too. Maybe not you specifically, but someone else."

"Let's cut the shit, Finn." She moved the mug across the table and black coffee sloshed around inside nearly going over the rim. "I don't buy your book research for a second. I want to know why you're really looking for them and you're going to tell me."

"Looking for *them*? So you do have Turner."

She smirked.

"Why don't you tell me why the federal government is protecting two child killers? The US Marshals are responsible for finding fugitives and protecting informants in WITSEC, but Vance and Turner never testified against anyone. They were never a part of any federal case and aren't eligible for federal protection, so why are you hiding them?"

Valerie shifted in her seat and I could tell she wasn't prepared for the barrage of questions. She probably thought all she had to do was flash her badge and I'd walk away with my tail between my legs. And while that would be the smart thing for me to do, I rarely did the smart thing.

"Our involvement is none of your goddamn business."

"Want to know my theory?" I thought back to what Nell told me about Vance's father working for the Department of Justice. "I think Daddy Vance pulled some strings with the DOJ and got his son and Turner into the program. Gave them a new start. A new life free from the stigma of being a known child killer."

"It's not my job to question who gets what deal and why. But it is my job to keep you from finding them. And that's what I'm prepared to do."

"How? I've already found Vance. He's running a goddamn child-care center. A child killer working with children all day. Nice work, Uncle Sam."

"Stop fishing."

"I don't think I have it in me to bow out now. I'm already in Flower Mound and I kind of want to see this thing through. Plus, I really don't have anything better to do with my time."

"Then you're an idiot."

"I've been called worse. To my face." I smiled. "By my own family."

"This isn't a joke, Finn. I can't legally stop you from looking for them but I can damn sure make your life hell if you don't let up."

"How's that?"

"We're the government." She smiled for the first time. "We make bad things happen to people all the time."

She was right about that. I knew two people serving life sentences for murders they didn't commit, all thanks to the FBI. But I also didn't think she was prepared to go that far. Not yet anyway.

She stuffed the bulging file back into her purse. "Of course, I could just move Vance and make you jump through your hoops all over again. All it takes is a phone call."

"I don't think so."

She raised her eyebrows.

"Here's the way I see it," I said. "Vance has been living in anonymity for the past twenty-four years. The Josh Baker case is old and stale, at least to anyone outside of Parkersburg, West Virginia, and I don't think Vance is fearing for his life. We're not talking about some mobster who went under after testifying against his family. The threat levels on these two are pretty low. And Vance is established here. He's running a business. Probably got a good income. No, if you show up in a black van outside his home in the middle of the night and tell him you want to up and move him across the country because I'm looking for him, I bet he tells you to fuck off and goes back to bed."

"You have a theory for everything don't you?" She slid her mug across the table again and looked as though she might actually drink it. "And you're an arrogant shit too."

"I'd go with confident, but my father and ex-wife would probably lean your way." I took another sip. "Are you assigned to both of them? I figured they wouldn't be in the same city given they're not supposed to have contact with one another. But it wouldn't surprise me if they had the same handler."

She didn't say anything.

I raised my mug again and noticed the wedding ring on her left hand. "You have any children?"

"Two."

"And you're comfortable with what these two did? That they served eight years in some children's dorm and now they're free to live out their lives in anonymity?"

"They did their time. It's not my job to continue to persecute them."

"I guess not everyone feels the way you do."

"Maybe not, but I still have a job to do and I'm not going to let you or anyone else stop me from doing it. I'd prefer that you just turned around and went back to Ohio so we can both get on with our lives."

"I'm not going anywhere."

She looked like she wanted to strangle me across the table. "Then get used to seeing me."

"I look forward to it."

She stood up and slipped her purse back over her shoulder. For the first time I caught a glimpse of her service weapon tucked on her hip beneath her blue blazer. I sensed she flashed it for emphasis.

"If you're going to stay on me you might want to switch vehicles. I've already burned your Fusion. The silver SUV too."

"I'm glad we had this little chat, Finn. Good to know where we both stand." She walked to the cafe door but stopped and turned back. "And Finn?"

"Yeah?"

She smiled. "We don't have any silver SUVs."

She closed the door behind her, walked across the street, stepped into her car and drove off.

CHAPTER 19

I PULLED AWAY from the coffee shop scanning the street for a silver SUV or a blue Fusion. I didn't see either, but after my run-in with Valerie I now thought that everyone on the street was a potential tail. I shook off my paranoia and headed to Vance's childcare center. I felt a pressure in my stomach and considered running into a gas station bathroom to banish the three large coffees I had that morning, but the urge to meet Jacob Vance in person was too strong to pull over.

Ten minutes later I stood in front of the Tot Spot. It was a nice facility. A colorful playground with numerous climbing apparatus and rubber floor mats stood empty inside a fenced perimeter on the right side of the building. I walked through the double glass doors and was immediately hit with the sound of laughter. To my right about a dozen children played in a colorful room adorned with Dora the Explorer and Scooby Doo characters that stood as tall as me.

Maybe it was the fact I didn't have a kid with me or maybe it was my beard, which Albert swore made me look like a child predator, but whatever the reason two young women in blue shirts with Tot Spot logos swarmed me.

"Can I help you, sir?" asked one of the women. She looked to be in her early twenties, and according to the tag on her shirt her name was Megan.

"Yes, I'm interested in learning more about your childcare center. For my daughter."

"Are you looking for part-time or full-time care?"

"Full time. We recently moved here and I'd passed by your place a few times and wanted to stop in."

"How old is your daughter?"

I scanned the children playing in the next room. "She's four. Four and a half actually."

"Right this way. If you follow me I can show you around."

"Are you the owner?" I asked.

"No. Mr. Polling is in the office."

"I'd like to meet him too. To be honest, I don't love the idea of leaving my little girl with strangers and I'd like to meet whoever's name is on the door."

"Of course. I can give you a quick tour and then introduce you to Mr. Polling."

"That'd be great."

For the next ten minutes Megan showed me around the facility. She had long hair that was dyed a deep red with a few purple streaks throughout. She wore thick blacked-rimmed glasses and looked like she read a lot of comic books. Megan made a point to talk up the facility's educational approach to childcare and their peanut-free environment, but all I really cared about was meeting Vance. And using the bathroom. After showing me the place and giving me a blue folder stuffed with forms and brochures, a hand lightly tapped me on the shoulder. I turned around and stared at a man who introduced himself as Jake Polling.

Vance's handshake was tight and firm, as if he tried to overcompensate for his short stature—he was five-foot-six at the most. Unlike his blue-shirted staff, he wore tan khaki slacks, a brown belt and a white button-up shirt. He had missed one of his belt loops getting dressed this morning. Maybe he was in a rush to get to work. He sported a buzz cut and a fresh shave.

"I hear you're interested in our facility?"

"That's right."

"I'll leave you two to talk," said Megan.

Polling nodded and I watched as his eyes followed her ass out of the room.

"You live nearby?" he said.

"A few miles away. In the process of moving here. I came early. My wife and daughter will be here this weekend." Remembering I didn't have a wedding band on my finger, I shoved my left hand into my pocket.

He looked me over. "Is there anything I can tell you about our place that Megan didn't touch on?"

"What's security like? I'm a really protective parent. One of those dads who's afraid something bad is going to happen."

"I think that's every parent." He motioned where the children played. "Everyone on staff has passed a background check. State law. Most of the people who work here have been with the team for five years or more. And they're great with the kids."

"Do you have children?" I asked, noticing his bare ring finger.

"No. I don't. I guess I consider all of these little ones my kids."

"Ever have an abduction? From the facility?"

"God no!"

"There was one in our hometown a few years ago. Before we had kids. Someone walked into a daycare, grabbed a kid and took off. I think it was a custody battle thing. Between the mother and father."

"That would never happen here. Safety is our number one concern. After all the children have been checked in we lock the doors until pick up. No one can just walk in without an appointment."

"I did."

"Parents were still dropping off children when you arrived. We hadn't locked up yet. I assume Megan greeted you pretty quickly after you came in."

"She did."

"That's what they're trained to do. Spot unfamiliar faces."

"That's good. If someone snatched her away from me, I'm not sure what I'd do." He looked up at me and I thought I saw his jaw clinch slightly, like he was chewing gum. "When you're a parent it's all you think about. Your kid's safety."

He nodded. "I can assure you…" He stopped himself. "What's your daughter's name?"

"Caroline."

"I can assure you that Caroline would be safe and comfortable here. I'd love to meet her. Your wife too."

"We'll stop in soon." I held up the blue folder. "Until then, I guess I have some reading to do."

"Anything else I can answer for you?"

"No. You've given me exactly what I wanted. Thanks."

"Sure thing." He placed a hand on my shoulder and nudged me toward the door.

"Do you mind if I run into your bathroom before I head out? Too much coffee this morning."

"Sure." Polling directed me to the bathroom and then turned to speak with one of the other employees.

I walked into the bathroom and felt like a giant next to the low urinals and sinks. The bathroom was painted to look like a jungle. Tall trees, thick leaves and an array of jungle animals covered the walls. I stepped to the urinal and handled my business while a tiger, who looked to be painted by an art school dropout, watched me from the corner. I zipped my pants, buckled my belt and glanced up at the ceiling. That's when I saw it.

You have to be observant in this business, because it's usually something small, something most people overlook, that can make or break a case. Most people wouldn't notice a car tailing them. They're not focused on it. But I had. I noticed that Polling was sloppy. He missed a belt loop on his pants. Normally that would mean he was running late and dressed too quickly, but he wasn't running late. Otherwise he wouldn't have shaved. That takes time, and you don't shave when you're running late. But he did. I noticed that every one of Polling's staff was an attractive, young woman. Maybe he missed the belt loop in a back room instead of his home. I noticed the way Polling looked at Megan when she walked away. I noticed that Polling didn't wear a wedding ring. And I noticed the two smoke detectors on the bathroom ceiling.

I wasn't up to speed on the Texas building codes and didn't know if businesses were required to have smoke detectors in the bathrooms or not, but I was damn certain they didn't need more than one for a room that was smaller than one-hundred-square-feet.

I walked to the sink, turned on the water and washed my hands as I surveyed the ceiling through the mirror in front of me. One smoke detector was in the middle of the room, the other was directly over the only stall in the bathroom. I dried my hands and walked to the stall. I grabbed a piece of toilet paper, folded it into a square and raised it to my nose and took a better look at the unit above the stall.

It was a different make than the unit in the center of the room. That one had a small green light in the center, but the one above my head had no light. It was a cheap casing that most people would never notice, but I wasn't most people.

There are countless mail-order catalogues and websites that sell all sorts of surveillance equipment. GPS trackers, bug detectors, listening devices, hidden cameras and a ton of other gear. At one time or another I had probably used half the gear available, but I had never used a hidden camera to record a kid in a bathroom.

I walked out of the bathroom to see Polling talking to Megan next to the front door. As I approached he pressed a button on the wall, which unlocked the front door. He opened the door wide.

"Thanks for checking us out," said Megan. "Feel free to call us with any questions."

"I'll do that."

I passed by the two of them.

"Hope to see you again," said Polling.

"You definitely will."

CHAPTER 20

After I left Vance's childcare center I returned to my hotel room to consider my next move. Before I could think too long, I received an email from Cricket. He indicated he was "doing my job for me" and attached two files. I clicked open the first file to fine Jacob Vance staring at me. Not the real Jacob Vance, but the age progression image Cricket had outsourced for me. The image was dead-on, so much so I thought for a moment it was a photograph of the man I'd just spoken to at the Tot Spot. I didn't know much about age progression software, but I'd expected to receive an image that looked like Vance but was "off," like a corpse at a loved one's funeral where you know something looks different but you can't put your finger on exactly what it is.

I didn't think anything I received from Cricket would be helpful, but this image was dead-on. I rooted through my messenger bag until I found Vance's original booking photo from 1984 and held the two images side by side. Vance's posture and blank facial expression were the same in each photograph, as was the stripped shirt, which fit the younger Vance but looked out of place on the older version.

If Vance's image was so exact, would Turner's be as accurate?

I closed Vance's image and clicked open Turner's file. There I found a man I'd never seen before. Unlike Vance, computer-generated Turner wore a sad expression. His eyes looked directly at the camera, his mouth slightly open, and he looked confused, like he didn't know where he was.

I grabbed Turner's booking photo from my bag and compared the two. As with Vance, computer-generated Turner wore the same white T-shirt that his younger self wore in the booking photo. His expression was also the same. While Vance seemed smug and confident, Turner appeared lost and afraid.

Nell Richards had mentioned a psychiatrist who testified during the Baker trial said in cases like this there was usually a follower and a leader. Nell said her notes were locked away in the newspaper's archives and that she couldn't remember which boy played which role, but after seeing both boys' expressions I'm not sure I needed her notes. To me, Vance was the leader. Cool and collected in the photo, almost as if he expected to be caught. But Turner looked like he was only along for the ride, a ride he never really wanted to be on.

But Willie Baker didn't hire me to interpret Turner's feelings. He wanted his location. Time to find him.

Of all the information databases I have access to, the one I use the most is the DMV database. You can't beat it for locating people. By running a DMV search I can get a name, home address, birth date, physical description, outstanding criminal warrants. Everything I need to find someone. It helped me find Vance and I was confident it would do the same for Turner.

With most other databases you need a name, a social security number or some other marker to start with. But in addition to personal information, the DMV database also includes a database of images. I didn't need a name. I could use Turner's computer-generated image to run a search. I hadn't considered this before receiving the images from Cricket because I didn't think they would be a close enough match to their true appearance, but after seeing how accurate Vance's image was to the real thing it made sense that Turner's image might be accurate too. But was it accurate enough to get a hit from an image search?

DMVs operate on the state level, so when you get pulled over by the Ohio Highway Patrol they can run your Ohio license plate through the Ohio DMV and pull your Ohio record in a few seconds. Unfortunately, I didn't know where Turner called home and that meant I'd have to cast a wide net and look at all 50 states. It wasn't going to be as easy as stroking a few keys. It was going to take time, something I had plenty of.

I logged into the DMV database and uploaded the image of Turner that Cricket provided. Now, all I could do was wait. I printed out copies of Vance's and Turner's images, stuck them in my messenger bag and headed to my car. There was something I had to do before putting a bow on Jacob Vance.

CHAPTER 21

BEFORE I COULD SHIFT my focus completely to Turner I needed one last piece of intel on Vance. Willie Baker wanted Vance's location so he could send someone to kill him. I don't take hit jobs. I've had to pull a trigger or two, but it's always been in self-defense, or at least a preemptive strike. I don't set out to murder people and I don't consider myself a killer. I do understand that when I find people they usually aren't found again, but that's on someone else. The people I find have done something to get themselves into a mess. That's not on me.

The problem with a case like this is I had no idea who Willie was going to send in to clean up Vance's mess. He mentioned he'd hired a few other investigators, much cheaper investigators, who didn't turn up shit before he hired me. It reminded me of a comic strip I read years ago that showed two barbers who set up shop across the street from one another. One had a sign outside his shop that read "$5 haircuts." The barber across the street put out a sign that read "I fix $5 haircuts."

There was a possibility Willie might hire out the hit to a pro, or to some gangbanger who didn't know his ass from an assault rifle. I know people who would put a bullet in someone's head for six figures, but I also know you could find some high school kid who might do it for a new pair of high-tops. Of course the quality is going to differ because, just like haircuts, you get what you pay for. Who knew what Willie was going to do, and I didn't want to ask him because I didn't want to know. Plausible deniability.

What I did want to know was whether Vance lived alone or if there was something else in his home that could be a problem for whomever Willie sent in to mop up. Like a one-hundred-pound Rottweiler. Or a girlfriend. I couldn't shake the feeling that Megan, the girl from the Tot Spot, spent the night there from time to time. I needed to get inside and find out if there was an alarm system, how many toothbrushes were in the bathroom, whether there were any toys on the floor, who was getting mail delivered there, anything important. That type of intel would go a long way in making sure whomever Willie sent got in and out with no problems. And that's favorable for everyone involved, me included.

But I couldn't do any of that until Vance left. I figured he would still be at the daycare, but his Toyota was in the driveway. Maybe he came home for lunch, or maybe he knocked off early. I decided to park down the street and wait him out.

I grabbed the folders from my messenger bag and tossed the bag in the back so I could spread out the information on the passenger seat. I hoped the DMV search would turn up something on Turner, because I didn't have much else to go on. With Vance I had a solid place to start, his parents. But Turner's parents were long gone and he didn't have any siblings, so I had no real breadcrumbs to follow. The only lead I had for Turner was Kim Burton, his ex-girlfriend, but that lead had already burned out.

Thinking about Turner's ex-girlfriend got me thinking about my ex-wife. Brooke was the type of person who didn't like to screw around. She always let you know what was on her mind and she made big, life-changing decisions on the fly like she was picking out shampoo at Target. That's why she had laid it out on the line about giving our marriage another go. I can't say the idea didn't intrigue me, it did, but I was the much more cautious type. I'd rather take my time and make the right play instead of rushing something and having to deal with the fallout later.

The idea of being a bigger part of Becca's life got me more excited than the thought of waking up to Brooke every morning, not that I wouldn't enjoy that. I loved spending each weekend with Becca, but making that a permanent thing again got my pulse jumping.

This case also rattled me like none before. I never brought my work home and always tried to separate my family from my paycheck, but the Josh Baker case reminded me that bad shit happens to good people all the time. Sometimes evil walks in and takes a piece of your life away for no reason whatsoever. Willie Baker seemed like a good guy, and his son was as innocent as they came. Vance and Turner had no motive for swiping that kid from the mall other than a morbid curiosity to see what would happen. What if that curiosity walked down my street someday and what if I wasn't there to stop it?

I knew I would have to deal with Brooke when I finished up with Vance and Turner, and I wasn't sure what I wanted to do. What I did know was I didn't need Brooke clouding my head when I should be sharp, so I pushed her out of my thoughts and returned to the case.

That's when the aluminum baseball bat shattered my passenger window, spraying glass across the inside of my Navigator. I instinctively lunged for the .45 tucked under my seat, but my seatbelt restrained me. I struggled to disengage the seatbelt, ready to kick open the driver door if I had to, when the bat slammed into my right shoulder. I turned to see Jacob Vance staring at me through the shattered window.

"Who the fuck are you?" He poked the tip of the bat into my

shoulder like he was pushing me off a ledge. "You're the guy from this morning."

My brain aimlessly searched for a bat-proof response, something to rationalize why I was sitting across the street from his home.

"What were you doing at my business today? And what are you doing here? At my house?"

Before I could conjure a response Vance reached in and poached the two photographs from my passenger seat, shook the glass shards off and studied them.

"Where did you get these?" After I didn't answer he raised the bat as high as he could inside the vehicle and struck my shoulder again. There was a dull thud and a sharp pain that radiated across my collarbone and down my arm. He cocked his swing again, smacking the rearview mirror as he drew his arm back, and slammed into my shoulder a third time. Had it not been for the limited range of motion inside the vehicle, which lessened the blow, he would have easily dislocated my shoulder. He drew the bat back again.

"Okay," I said. "Stop with the bat!"

"Talk or the next one comes at your face. Why are you looking for me?"

"You're a smart guy, Jacob. Why do you think?"

"That was a long time ago. It doesn't mean shit now."

"It means something to some people."

As he looked at the photos again I reached out and seized the bat, pulling him forward into the passenger door. He dropped the photos on the passenger seat, snapped his arms back outside the vehicle and braced himself on the door.

"Why are you looking for me? You working for a magazine or newspaper or something? Want to show my picture to everyone? Out me as a killer? You can't write a goddamn thing. I'm still protected by the courts. You run a story and I'll sue the shit out of you and your paper."

"That's not true. You should brush up on the law, but it doesn't matter anyway, because I'm not writing anything Jacob. Just curious what happens to a guy like you when he grows up."

Vance leaned back inside the car. "Curiosity can get you killed, you know? I'd think twice about that before poking your nose into shit that doesn't concern you."

"I'll keep that in mind."

Vance pulled his head out of the passenger window and looked up and down the street before ducking back in. "You think I'm just going to sit here and let you spy on me? No way. If I see you again, anywhere, I'll cave your fucking head in." He reached for the bat but I jerked it away from him. "And you and I both know I'm capable of doing it."

Vance drove his foot into my side fender and then stormed across the street to his SUV. He sped passed me as I waited for the feeling to return to my shoulder and arm. I used one of Willie's file folders to brush the glass shards from the passenger seat onto the floor.

That's when I noticed my printouts of Vance's and Turner's age-progression photos were gone.

CHAPTER 22

OVER THE PAST two days I'd suffered a car accident-induced headache and a nearly broken arm and shoulder thanks to a Louisville Slugger knockoff. I wasn't sure if my car or my body paid the greater price, but at this pace neither would survive the week. I decided to head to my hotel to nurse my wounds and see if my DMV search had found any records connected to Turner's image.

When I returned to my room the five worst words in the PI dictionary greeted me: your search found no matches. I'd hoped to get a hit on the DMV search using Turner's age-progression image, but something in the back of my head told me not to be optimistic.

Just because I didn't get a match didn't mean Turner wasn't in the system. My gut told me it was the photo. Just because Vance looked like his computer-generated alter ego didn't mean Turner did. He could look completely different. Maybe he had a beard or a mustache or wore glasses. Maybe Turner didn't have a driver's license and wasn't in the DMV system at all. Or maybe he dropped dead years ago and was kicked out of the system.

My arm throbbed like hell and felt like I had been lying on it for hours. I grabbed a plastic liner from the trashcan and filled it with ice at the icemaker down the hall. I tied off the bag, wrapped it with a towel, placed it on my right bicep and hoped the pain would die down.

A few minutes later my phone buzzed.

"You get the photos?" asked Cricket.

"I had them."

"What do you mean had?"

"Never mind. So far I haven't had any luck with 'em."

"What you try?"

"I already found Vance, but I took your image of Turner and ran it through the DMV. I hoped I'd get a hit on him with just his image."

"Doubt that would work."

"The image you gave me for Vance was dead-on. Figured if Turner's was as accurate something might pop."

"But you didn't get a hit, because you're looking in the wrong place. Too many variables for a DMV search. If his face is the slightest bit different, you won't find shit."

I could sense Cricket's smug expression through the phone. "All right Columbo, where should I look?"

"ATMs."

I didn't know where he was going with the ATM angle, and from my long silence Cricket must have realized that.

"Skimmers have been a big thing lately," he continued. "People sticking skimmers on ATMs to capture your account numbers as you withdraw cash. The banks have been using facial recognition for fraud prevention for a while, but it's been a closed network. If Bank A gets a call about fraudulent activity at one of its ATMs, the security guy can run through footage at a specific ATM. If he sees video evidence of someone placing a skimmer on the unit the bank can run the guy's facial image through its own ATM image database and see if he's hitting any of their other machines."

"I didn't know that was a thing."

"Most people don't," he said. "It's one of those Big Brother-ish things you wish didn't exist. Until you need to use it."

"I didn't realize you were so tech-savvy."

"Got to stay up on trends, Finn. To keep people like you coming back."

"But if it's a closed network then the bank could only search its own ATMs and I've got no idea where this guy is banking. I don't even know what state he's in."

"That's where the government comes in. Uncle Sam has been working with banks to connect all the systems so they have a single database of images. All in the name of public safety. Imagine how pissed off people would be if the government started spying on people all over the country. Cameras on every street corner, that sort of thing. Now they don't have to. They can use a system that's already in place—ATMs. They're not on every street corner, but they're damn close."

"How accurate is it?"

"It's not like the DMV, if that's what you're asking. People can change their appearance, but this thing looks for the stuff you can't change. The distance between your pupils, how long your nose is or the length of your lips. Real James Bond shit."

"But that assumes my guy is using an ATM," I said. "What if he isn't?"

"When was the last time you were at an ATM, Finn?"

"Last week."

"I was at one this morning," said Cricket. "Everyone uses them. If your guy has been to an ATM in the last five years, he's in the database. And if we match his face, we can get his bank accounts, and more importantly, whatever name he's using."

"Why in the hell didn't you mention this earlier? You could have saved me some time."

"I didn't want to meddle in your shit. Plus, I thought you could find him using more conventional ways. But I guess not."

"How do I get into the system?" I said.

"You don't, but I can. It ain't cheap."

"Nothing with you ever is." I didn't have to think about it. "Run the search and let me know what you get. How long will it take?"

"I'll get back to you tomorrow morning."

I hung up the phone and relaxed on the bed with my icepack and a renewed optimism that I might have Turner's identity when the sun came up.

CHAPTER 23

THE NEXT MORNING I woke up at 5:45 to a dog barking in the hotel parking lot. It sounded like a small dog, one someone might shove into a purse. It took a moment to realize I had slept in a puddle of water from my melted icepack. I rolled out of bed, threw on my clothes and looked out the window, half tempted to go after the dog and search for a snooze button. What I saw was my Navigator with a busted passenger window frowning back at me. I didn't know how much longer I would be on the road, but I'd have to patch that up until I got home.

After grabbing breakfast I picked up a blue tarp to go with the roll of duct tape I already had and sealed the gaping window. I was on my way back to my hotel when I saw the blazing red and blue lights of a police cruiser behind me. No siren. I pulled to the side of the road and he stopped several car lengths behind me. I sat with my hands at ten and two watching the police officer in my rearview mirror. He sat in his cruiser longer that I thought he would.

My watch said I'd been idling on the side of the road for seven minutes, more than enough time for him to run my plates, and still no visit. Finally, he stepped from his car, put his right hand on his hip and approached the passenger side of my vehicle. He wore a white cowboy hat that seems large enough to hide an armadillo.

I rolled down the rear passenger window since the tarp covered the passenger front.

"Afternoon," he said from behind me. "Can you step out of the car please?"

"There a problem?"

"Not yet."

I learned a long time ago that it was fruitless to argue with a police officer at a traffic stop. He had already made up his mind that he wanted me out of the car and there wouldn't be anything I could say or do to keep that from happening. I disengaged my seatbelt, opened the driver's door and stepped out. I placed my hands on the roof and bent down so I could see him through the window.

"What seems to be the problem?" I said, trying to figure out what I had done to warrant a personal conversation.

He walked around the front of my Navigator and surveyed the damage. "What the hell happened here?"

"Some woman slammed into me the other day. It's still roadworthy."

"You figure on getting it fixed?"

"At some point. When I get back to," I stopped short of revealing my hometown. "When I get home."

"She really did a number on you. You hit a pothole the right way and your whole front end is liable to fall off."

"I'm hoping that doesn't happen, sir."

"What are you doing in Texas?"

"I'm a private investigator and I'm working a case down here."

"You have a weapon on you?"

"No." It wasn't a lie because my .45 was tucked inside my messenger bag back in my hotel room. I didn't like the fact he hadn't explained why he stopped me. "What's this about officer? My front end?"

He lowered his chin to his chest and peered at me over his sunglasses. I couldn't see his hands, but I assumed one of them rested on his weapon. "I'm going to need you to come with me."

"How's that?"

"Just need to talk to you and I'd rather not do it on the side of the street with traffic tearing by."

I was curious whether he planned on taking me for a drive. I knew the law and could refuse to get out of my car if I wanted to. I had the right to remain inside my vehicle unless he planned on arresting me, but while that was my legal right, I could tell by the no-shit-taking grin in his face that I would be getting out of the vehicle one way or another.

"Do I need to lock up my vehicle?"

"Nope."

As I walked toward his cruiser he circled around behind me but stayed several feet back.

"It's open," he said.

I pulled on the rear door handle, opened the door and climbed into the back seat. He checked his watch, but didn't get into the cruiser. That didn't surprise me because he hadn't frisked me, and no cop in his right mind would sit in front of me without knowing he was unarmed.

A moment later a familiar blue Fusion pulled up behind the cruiser and Deputy Marshal Valerie Cheatham stepped out of the car, patted the officer on the shoulder and opened the door I'd just crawled through minutes earlier.

"Got room for one more?" she said, climbing in and ushering me to the other side of the seat.

"This a welcome-to-Texas thing?" I said.

"We already had that conversation at the coffee shop. This is a why-didn't-you-fucking-listen-to-me thing."

"Right."

"I hoped our chat yesterday might make you reconsider your

vacation down here, but then I hear you went to Vance's place of business. That right?"

"That's right."

"What you'd say to him?"

"Nothing really. Just wanted to meet him face-to-face."

"He's not some carnival sideshow freak or a tourist attraction." She shook her head. "How'd you find him?"

"Trade secret."

"You tell anyone about what you found?"

That was the type of question someone gets asked right before they take a bullet in the head. But I was confident Valerie wasn't going to off me in the back of a police cruiser on a Texas highway.

"Not yet," I said.

She nodded. "You must be pretty good at your job. Shame about the license and all."

"Shit happens," I said

"Want it back?"

"What?"

Valeria pulled a white envelope from behind her and handed it to me. I opened it. Inside was an official letter recommending the reinstatement of my PI license in thanks for my dedicated service to the US Marshals. It had a fancy seal and was signed by the US Marshal's Director for the Northern District of Texas.

"What the hell is this?"

"Consider it a buyout. Just turn that letter in to the Ohio Department of Public Safety and you get your PI license back. No questions asked. All you have to do is walk away from all this and forget what you know. Just walk away and you get your old life back."

"Who says I want it back?"

"Come on. My guess is since getting finger fucked by the state and losing your license you've been reduced to taking shit jobs to make ends meet."

"I do pretty well for myself."

"Yeah, but at what expense? Your client list is probably full of stupid fucks who think they're above the law. The kind of people who don't last too long and can drag you down with them. You pick the wrong case or work for the wrong guy and someone puts two in the back of your head and leaves you in an abandoned basement somewhere. It's not a solid long-term strategy. And what would your daughter think about what you do? She's what, eight now? Shouldn't you be a better role model?"

"Looked into me, huh?"

"It's what we do."

I placed the letter back into the white envelope and folded it in half. "I'll have to think about your proposal."

"Think about it long and hard. I can't sit back and let you undermine the WITSEC program. This is your last chance to walk away with your dick intact." She tapped the envelope with a perfectly painted fingernail. "This is all I can give you, Finn. The next time we meet, I'll start taking things away."

"The next time? Who says you'll be able to find me again?"

"Jesus Christ. You're driving a piece of shit SUV with a blue tarp for a window. It won't take Scotland Yard to find you."

She rapped her knuckle on the window and the police officer opened the door. She climbed out and I followed.

"And Finn."

"Yeah?"

"Remember when we were in the coffee shop and you mentioned something about a silver SUV?"

"And you said it wasn't yours."

"It's not ours. But I've seen it a few times since our chat. Ran the plate too."

"You going to tell me who it is?"

She shook her head. "Trade secret."

I cracked a smile and started toward my SUV. I was halfway there when she called out to me.

"Remember Finn, this was a friendly meeting. The next one won't be."

I pretended not to hear her over the passing highway traffic and opened my car door. Once inside, I stuck the envelope under my sun visor, fired the engine and pulled into traffic.

I WASN'T A QUARTER MILE AWAY FROM THE STILL-PARKED POLICE cruiser when my cell buzzed. It was Cricket.

"You're up early," I said. "I took you for the type of person who slept in."

"No one accomplished anything by sleeping in. I've got good news for you."

"I could use some good news. And a new window. And a fender."

"What?"

"Never mind."

"Listen," he said. "My friend ran the photo through the bank surveillance system and we got a match. His name is Ray Asher and his last ATM transaction was a week and a half ago at a bank in Dallas."

"Well that's convenient as shit," I said.

"How's that?"

"I'm about forty minutes away. It can't be a coincidence that he's in the same area as Vance. How sure are you this is Ray Turner, the kid in the original photo?"

"You got any better leads?"

"No."

"Then don't shit on this until you've checked it out. I've seen the ATM image and it's a close hit to the age-progression photo. This isn't an exact science, but it's damn close. The fact his face matches the key markers from the photo and that he's in the same area as your other mark... Like you said, it can't be a coincidence."

"Fingers crossed."

"I'll email you his banking information from the system. You can take it from there."

I thanked Cricket, clicked off my phone and headed back to the hotel.

CHAPTER 24

TEXAS WAS the last place I expected to find Raymond Turner. I initially thought the DOJ would relocate the two as far away from one another as possible, but the more I thought about it the more it made sense. Flower Mound and Dallas were thirty miles apart. That doesn't seem that far, but considering the Dallas-Fort Worth-Arlington region was the fourth most populated metro area in the country, the odds of Vance and Turner bumping into each other was statistically improbable.

Aside from the number of cowboy boots around, there was another benefit to keeping them in the same area. My gut told me that my new friend at the US Marshals was responsible for both Vance and Turner, and what better way to stay on top of them than by checking in with them in person. Keeping them at arm's length made Valerie's job easier. It made my job easier too.

Before I went after Turner, I had to confirm he and Ray Asher indeed shared a heartbeat. My first attempt at finding Turner through the DMV database was a bust, but that was when I only had a digital doppelgänger to work with. Now I had something more solid. The bank account information that Cricket sent included Ray Asher's social security number, which I traced. It didn't take long to discover the Social Security Administration assigned Ray Asher his digits the same month and year as Jake Polling, the same time they left Pleasant Hill. The discrepancy in his birthdate was also consistent with Polling's womb emancipation day—exactly one month later than those of their real birthdates. I had my guy.

I ran an employment search, which revealed Ray Asher led an aptly named charity, The Raymond Asher Foundation. A quick Internet search took me to the organization's homepage. I wasn't sure what to expect, but I didn't expect that Ray Asher, formerly Raymond Turner, ran a charity helping missing and exploited children in Texas.

You've got to be shitting me.

By my own estimation Jacob Vance was a piece of shit, and not just because he customized the inside of my Navigator with a baseball bat. Given his past, I didn't like the idea of Vance having daily contact with children at his childcare center. Turner, on the other hand, actively helped missing and abused children. At least that's what his organization's glossy website told me. Was Turner helping disadvantaged children in an attempt to atone for what he did to Josh Baker? I wasn't a firm believer that people changed, especially people who murder children, but I was willing to give him the benefit of the doubt. For now.

The bank account information Cricket sent included the mailing address Turner used to open his account, but the only way to confirm whether it was current was to pay him a visit. I scribbled down his home and business addresses in my notepad, grabbed my messenger bag and the only suit I brought with me and walked to the hotel parking lot.

I could make it to Dallas by 8 a.m.

DESPITE MY BEST EFFORTS TO SEAL UP MY SHATTERED PASSENGER window with the tarp, my SUV whistled the forty miles from

Flower Mound to Turner's home in Dallas. I considered renting a vehicle for the remainder of my time in Texas, but I couldn't rent a car under an alias since I didn't have an insurance card for anyone other than Finn Harding. And even though Valerie could place me in Flower Mound, I didn't want a paper trail to back up her account. So that meant suffering with the wailing Navigator until I made it back to a Cincinnati body shop.

The GPS took me across SH 114 east to I-35E and then to Turner's home on Molly Court, which was about ten miles south of Dallas. It was a nice place for a child killer. Red brick with black shutters, a side garage and a better view than Josh's burial vault. It was a federal style with a flat front and lots of windows. It was the kind of home you wanted to live next to. The kind that drives up everyone's home values in the neighborhood. Apparently Turner's federal aid package paid higher than Vance's did.

I had only been there twenty minutes when a black minivan pulled out of the garage and onto the street. I got a quick glance before it made a right turn away from me, but it was long enough to see a male, who I assumed was Turner, in the driver's seat. I gave him some distance and then pulled out behind him.

Fifteen minutes after leaving his home Turner pulled the minivan into a parking lot and stopped in front of the Adelle Lee Elementary School. I parked on the street and watched as a tall thin brunette stepped out of the passenger side of the vehicle, slid open the side door and escorted two young girls into the building, waving to a parking lot attendant as she passed. Five minutes later she climbed back into the SUV and they pulled onto the street. I did the same.

After another fifteen minutes Turner pulled into a building complex. I checked my notepad. The address wasn't Turner's foundation. The minivan parked in front of a large, modern, gray building with enough glass windows to reduce the city's bird population by at least fifty percent. The woman stepped out of the minivan again, this time with a briefcase in her hand. She walked around to the driver's door and kissed Turner though the open window. Turner waited for her to walk inside the building before pulling away.

I continued the routine and followed the minivan until it pulled into a strip mall. Turner parked, walked across the lot and stepped through a glass door with a black and white sign over it. The Raymond Asher Foundation. The office was small and had probably once been a Radio Shack. It sat wedged between a tobacco store and a tax preparer's office.

Thanks to my unorthodox career I rarely wore suits. When I was a licensed PI I often had to take the witness stand in court, and that meant slapping on a shirt that was too tight around my neck and a tie that I never knotted exactly right. Of all the things I missed from being a legitimate PI, wrapping my six-foot-one frame in a suit wasn't one of them. But I had to suit up for my conversation with Turner. Otherwise, he'd never believe I was telling the truth when I lied to his face.

There was a gas station across the street from Turner's strip mall. I left the parking lot, stopped in front of the gas station, grabbed my suit and stepped inside. I traded my jeans and button-up blue shirt for a charcoal gray suit inside the bathroom, ordered a to-go cup of coffee and left the college-aged attendant scratching her head as to why I changed into a suit in her bathroom. Not a common practice.

I retuned to the strip mall parking lot, found a spot at the far end of the lot, checked my crooked tie in the rearview mirror, took the leather portfolio I kept stashed in the backseat and went to see Turner.

An electronic sensor chimed like a kid's toy with a dying battery as I walked into the building. Inside, the Raymond Asher Foundation resembled a local upstart politician's campaign headquarters. The building was divided into two sections. The front section contained a large table surrounded by six cubicles, only three of which were occupied. One wall held a large map of Texas. It looked like something you'd find at an interstate welcome center. The other wall had a white board that hung over a lateral file cabinet. Next to that stood a wooden rack of brochures. There was an office in the rear of the building that was separated from the front room by a large glass partition. Inside was a man, who I assumed was Ray Turner, in a white button-up shirt leaning over a desk. There was a door to the right of his desk that, given its placement in the room, I guessed led out to the rear parking lot.

Before I could get too far inside the building, a young man approached and asked how he could help.

"I'd like to speak with Ray Asher," I said. "Is he available?"

He looked over his shoulder toward the office. "Just a second. Let me see if he's off the phone." The young man walked to the rear office, knocked on the partition and said something to Asher. A moment later both men returned.

"I'm Raymond Asher."

There was no mistaking that Raymond Asher was the man in the age-progression photo Cricket sent me. I stood eye-to-eye with Ray Turner. Aside from the way he styled his hair—slicked back and parted over to the side like a Wall Street banker—he looked identical to his younger, child-murdering self.

"Hello. I'm Roger Mathers," I said. "Is there some place we can talk?"

"Sure," said Turner. "Is everything all right?"

"Everything is great and it might get better."

Turner arched his brow and flashed a nervous smile. "Okay. We can talk in my office."

I could feel the staff watching us as he led me to the office. Once inside, he took a chair from next to a small table and slid it to the center of the room. I sat down and he took a seat behind his desk.

"What can I do for you?" he asked.

I crossed my legs and set the leather portfolio on my lap.

"I represent a gentleman who is interested in making a large donation to your organization and I'm here on his behalf to assess your operation and advise him whether that's a good idea or not."

"What kind of donation?"

"The six-figure kind."

He leaned forward in his swivel chair. "Can you tell me who it is?"

"No. He'd like to remain anonymous. But he does have an interest in what you do and would like to see you do even more."

"We'll, we're a small operation. We should probably do more outreach for donations, but to be honest, I'm not comfortable asking people for money. We operate mostly on a grant from the state and from donations from a few individuals. I can count them on one hand, so we'd be very appreciative of anything your friend could donate. Is there anything specific I can share?"

"My associate likes to back people who are passionate about what they do and that's really why I'm here. We've already vetted your organization as a whole, but I'm more interested in learning more about you. Why you're here, why you do this. The kind of information you can't get from an annual report."

"Well I started this organization about twenty years ago because I want to help kids. It's cliché, but I wanted to help people who can't help themselves. Adults usually end up in bad situations because of their own decisions, but children are different. Most of the things that happen to them aren't a consequence of their own actions, but rather someone else's."

"Why didn't you just go work for one of the bigger charities that helps children? You'd have more money to work with. Why go out on your own?"

"There are a lot of good organizations out there that do what we do on a grander scale, but only a small chunk of their budget goes to actual programs. Those organizations are still doing good, but I didn't want a third of my budget going to operations. I want to reinvest everything I can into programs." He pointed to the front of the building. "That's why we're in this space. Sure I could rent space in a nice office complex, but that's more money, money that could be going to help get kids off the street, or help reunite a lost child with their family, or helping educate teens about online predators. For me, it's all about the programs. All about doing something that really makes an impact."

I leaned forward. "How did you get here Mr. Asher? It's my experience that people in this type of work have a personal connection to it. Something that ignited their passion. Did you have a personal connection to a case or something? Maybe your own personal tragedy?"

Turner stared at me. He took a drink from a green plastic water bottle on his desk and wiped his mouth with the back of his hand.

"I can't point to one specific thing that led me down this path. Just a desire to help people."

I waited for him to say something else, but he didn't.

"You have a family?" I said.

"Yes, I'm married with two daughters. Twins. They're seven."

"And you're the one who runs the organization? You call the shots?"

"I have a board of advisors, but I'm the only executive. I develop all the programming and handle staffing. We have a small staff, but only one is salaried. Besides myself. The others are all volunteers. I'm not the only one passionate about helping children around here."

"Tell me about the passion. What are you most proud of?"

"It sounds mundane, but we run a 24-hour help line where teens can call if they need to talk to someone. About anything. We've had a lot of success there because a lot of kids are too afraid to talk to their parents and we give them an outlet. Recently we've been focused on educating parents and children about Internet safety. We've seen a significant increase in the number of teens assaulted by people they've met online. Given the sexual nature of the crimes, it's almost exclusively young girls. We do a lot of speaking at schools throughout the state, talking about how students can protect themselves online and letting them know we're here to help."

I tapped the portfolio on my lap. "I can see why you're passionate about that. I have a young daughter myself and I don't know what I'd do if someone hurt her. I'm sure that's a feeling every father faces. What to do with someone who hurts their kid."

Turner nodded and took another drink. "I suppose so."

"What about missing children?"

He stared at me and then stood up.

"Come on," he said. "I want to show you something."

Turner led me out of the office to the front of the building. He opened the top drawer of the lateral file cabinet, reached in and tossed a folder onto the table in the middle of the room.

"These are some of the people we've helped over the years," he said, opening the folder and spreading photos across the table.

I stood behind Turner as he plucked one at random from the pile. "This boy here. His name is Kevin. He was living with his father not too far from here. His mother kidnapped him a year ago last June. She abducted him because she lost custody in the courts. We hired a private investigator, who tracked her to a crack house in Cleveland. We worked with Cleveland police, who went in and got him, and we reunited Kevin with his father. He's an honor student now. And he has a real future."

He tossed the photo back on the pile and picked up another.

"This is Tara. She was a runaway. We found her living under a bridge in Garland, eating scraps she found in garbage cans. I went to visit her twice a week for three months. Brought her clothes and food. And I talked to her. She refused to go home because she was afraid of her father, but I convinced her to let me drive her to a homeless shelter here in Dallas. She lived there for two years, got back on her feet, and even got a job. Now she lives in an apartment with a friend. She's living in a safe environment, she's healthy and she's self-sufficient. She also volunteers at high schools around the area talking about her experience."

He lobbed the photo on top of the others.

"These kids are thriving today because of our efforts. I'm not trying to sound high-and-mighty, but sometimes these kids fall through the cracks and we're doing everything we can to keep that from happening. One kid at a time."

I looked up to find three employees standing next to a cubicle wall watching Turner. Their expressions—tight lips and wide eyes—told me they respected him and that they'd follow him into battle, no matter where he asked them to go or what he asked them to do.

Turner shook his head. "Whenever I get too stressed out or on those nights that I'm so busy that I sleep on the floor in my office, that's when I open this folder. This is what it's all about. These are the tangible results of what we're doing." He pushed the photos back into the folder and placed the folder back into the file cabinet. "This is what really matters. Every one of these kids has a story, and I like to think it's a better story because of us."

He turned around and his staff darted back into their cubicles.

"It seems like you're doing a lot of good work here, Mr. Asher."

"Thank you." He slipped his wallet out of his rear pants pocket, opened it and handed me a business card. "That's my direct line. Let me know if there is anything else I can tell you. Or your associate. I'm not like a politician and I don't really know how to ask for money, but we do have some wonderful programs and any donation would help us expand on the good we're already doing."

I shook Turner's hand and walked out of the building.

Karma is bullshit. The idea that it all evens out in the end is crap, a fairy tale we tell ourselves to help cope with all the bad shit people get away with. Turner seemed committed to helping people. I guess that's good for something. I wasn't sure if he believed his organization's efforts made up for crushing a four-year-old's skull with rocks, but unlike Vance, Turner seemed to be making an attempt to right his past wrongs.

I walked across the parking lot and climbed into my Navigator more conflicted than I was thirty minutes ago. I opened the folder on my passenger seat and snatched a photo. It wasn't an image of a runaway or some kid living in a crack house. It was Turner. Taken a few days after he murdered Josh Baker. He held a small whiteboard with his name and booking date and he stared at the camera with a dazed, lost expression, a far cry from the confident and determined face he wore when he regaled me with stories of the kids he'd saved.

When I walked into Turner's office I was determined to sign his death warrant. Now, I wasn't sure I should.

I PLACED TURNER'S PHOTO BACK INTO THE FOLDER AND SLIPPED IT inside my messenger bag underneath my .45. I reached for my keys in the console cup holder. That's when someone in the backseat slipped a clear plastic bag over my head and jerked me backward, pinning me against the driver's seat. I was usually aware of my surroundings, and glancing into the backset was the first thing I did before I climbed into my car. I must have gotten complacent once I crossed the Texas state line and I hoped it didn't get me killed. I made a deal with myself that if I survived this, I wouldn't let it slip again.

My instinct took over and I swatted widely at the thick forearm trying to break his grip on the bag, but he only clenched tighter. I had just taken a breath before I saw the bag and figured I had about thirty-seconds before the lights went out. I drove my right elbow backward and connected with something, but he didn't loosen his grip on the bag. As I kept striking backward with my right elbow, I opened my mouth wide and tried to gouge a hole in the bag with my left thumb but I couldn't tear through the thick lining. Whoever was in the back seat reached around and slammed a fist into my stomach and I immediately exhaled what was left in my lungs. I felt the warm air on my face as my breath escaped my lips and fogged up the inside of the bag. I slid my right hand down to the console and found my keys in the cup holder. I opened my mouth wide and stabbed a key through the bag, tasting the metal key on my tongue. I gasped. My chest expanded and fresh air rushed in.

With renewed strength, I drove my elbow back again but didn't connect with anything. Then I reached across to the passenger seat and clutched my .45 inside my bag. As I pulled it out, a hand seized my wrist, jerked it backward behind the passenger seat and twisted. I felt something pop and waited for my elbow to dislocate, but before it snapped he released the bag, reached a hand underneath the driver's headrest, wrapped his fingers around the side of my neck and drove my head into the driver's window. My head struck the window three times before I blacked out.

When I came to the bag was still draped loosely over my head and whoever had been in the backseat was gone. I pulled the bag off and checked my head for damage. Aside from the thin stream of blood trickling down the side of my face and beard, I was in one piece. I picked up my .45 from the floor in the backseat and scanned the parking lot for anyone who could have been behind me minutes earlier. Nothing.

My right arm felt like it had repeatedly been crushed in an oven door and the entire left side of my face throbbed like a ten-year-old boy who found his first *Playboy*.

Whoever was in the backseat didn't want me dead, but they did want to send me a message. I doubted Vance could have followed me to Dallas, and had it been him in the backseat he probably would have finished the job. I looked around for my car keys and that's when I saw the business card sitting on my steering column.

Valerie Cheatham, Deputy Marshal.

CHAPTER 25

Valerie Cheatham had warned me to stop digging into Vance and Turner, but if I made a habit of doing what others told me to do I'd be in a different line of work. It was not illegal to look for someone and Valerie had no authority to yank me off the street. She had, however, slipped a noose around my neck and was slowing tightening it. I didn't plan on being around when she gave it a final jerk. Her willingness to hire a thug to beat me unconscious inside my own vehicle told me she was as committed to hiding Vance and Turner as I was to finding them. That meant I didn't have a lot time to wrap things up.

Despite what some thought of me, I did have a moral compass. It didn't always point north, but it was there. Someone had to pay for Josh Baker's murder, but it didn't have to be Turner. After staring into his eyes and hearing about what he did to help those kids, I wasn't convinced he needed to die. It's not my job to forgive or judge people, but I did have a thumbs-up or thumbs-down vote on whether Turner kept breathing. And since I figured more children would benefit from a world that included Raymond Turner, my thumb was leaning north.

Willie knew nothing about Turner. I could tell him that I uncovered Turner's new identity, but that he had died years ago. Willie didn't seem like the type who would want to know all the details of Turner's life. He just wanted him found and he wanted him dead. I could give Willie a fake name and fabricated death certificate and he would never know the truth. Ray Asher goes on living and helping people and Willie goes on assuming Raymond Turner punched out and had to deal with his sins in the afterlife. Win, win.

Vance on the other hand was a dead man. Willie could have him. But that meant retrieving the two age-progression photos Vance lifted from my Navigator after he broke my window and introduced me to his aluminum baseball bat. I didn't want those laying around when the evidence team bagged the contents in Vance's house after his impending murder.

Since Valerie was Vance's handler, the local PD would include her in the investigation. It wouldn't take long for my name to come up. My name crossing Valerie's lips didn't worry me, but if anyone found my prints on those photos I'd be treading shit. The FBI already had my prints on file from a previous case and Valerie knew that, so if those photos showed up at his house it wouldn't take long for the investigators to make a match and link me to his residence.

Time to return to Flower Mound.

I DROVE PAST VANCE'S HOUSE AROUND NOON AND DIDN'T SEE HIS Toyota SUV in the driveway. My vehicle, with its shattered bumper and blue tarp window grew more conspicuous by the day, another reason to put a bow on this case and get back home. I parked five blocks down the street, slipped a pair of blue nitrile gloves into my pocket and walked to Vance's house on Sycamore Street.

Vance's house looked out of place next to his neighbors. The house was white with mold growing on the north side and grass that was a few inches taller than it should be. Two metal kitchen chairs sat on the front porch, one on its side.

I rounded the block and approached the house from the back. The houses on Sycamore stood close together. There was maybe ten feet between the sides of Vance's house and those on either side. A sun-bleached storm cellar door with a thick padlock led to Vance's basement. I didn't carry a lock pick set, but I did have three paper-clips in my wallet that I could use in a pinch. Thanks to the cellar door's rusty hinges though, I didn't need them. After glancing around to make sure no one was watching me, I slipped on my gloves, worked my fingers underneath the bottom edge of the door near the ancient lower hinge and heaved. The rusted screws pulled free from the door molding with a screech. I moved my hands to the top of the door and did the same thing. A few seconds later I raised the side edge high enough that I could sneak inside.

Once in the basement, I carefully lowered the cellar door back into place behind me and headed for the main floor. The basement had a concrete floor, cinderblock walls and smelled like frat house carpet. At the end of the room, six wooden steps and a flaking white door led up to the main floor.

As I approached the door, I passed a washer and dryer and a warped storage shelves made from 2x4s and plywood. Next to that was the entrance to another basement room. A blue tarp, a larger version of the one covering my passenger window, hung from the ceiling, concealing the room. Twine knots tied to rusted grommets held it in place. But whoever hung it didn't hang it straight and I could see a sliver of darkness behind it. I normally wouldn't have paid it much attention, but I noticed several electrical cords running from an outlet next to the washer underneath the tarp into the other room. Something about those cords wouldn't let me dismiss it, even though a voice inside my head told me to stop screwing around and get to finding the photos I had come for. I told the voice to fuck off and ducked my head past the tarp and clicked on my mobile phone's flashlight. What I saw on the other side hit me like food poisoning.

For a moment I thought I'd walked through a dingy portal into my old elementary school. There was a desk, a chalkboard, file cabinets, an American flag and an alphabet line tacked to a piece of yellow-painted drywall. It resembled a pristine representation of what a school classroom is supposed to look like. A piece of bright red carpet covered the gray concrete floor underneath. The perimeter of the room was dark and dirty, like a crawlspace in an abandoned amusement park. But the carpeted classroom in the middle of the room was clean, as if it had been set up yesterday. I turned and saw a video camera on a tripod, two industrial lighting stands, and three coat hangers holding neatly pressed school uniforms. Size small. Very small. It was a film set for a film I didn't want to know existed.

I stepped back through the crinkled curtain and pocketed my phone. I took the steps at the far end of the basement two at a time, opened the white door and stepped into a kitchen. I stood motionless, listening to hear if anyone else was in the house. The last thing I needed was to come face-to-face with a roommate who didn't park in the driveway. After listening to silence for a minute, I went to work.

I hoped to find the photos sitting on a counter in plain sight, but hope often shit on me and today was no different. I swept throughout the house like a hummingbird with its ass on fire, moving from the kitchen to the dining room to the living room and then upstairs to the three bedrooms, my boots thumping across the hardwood floor. I checked every drawer, cabinet and closet, but I didn't see the photos. Vance's house was small and I'd rummaged through both floors in about twenty minutes. Then I remembered there was a garage attached to the house. I went back downstairs to the kitchen and slipped through the door into the garage.

After yanking the pull string to the only light above me, I moved across the oil-splotched concrete floor to the workbench on the far wall. There, next to a rusted vice, were the photos. I folded them in half, crammed them into my back pocket, clicked off the light and went back into the kitchen.

On my way to the basement I passed a laptop sitting on the kitchen counter. The same voice that told me to skip the tarp-covered room in the basement urged me to leave the laptop behind and get out of the house, but I reached out, opened it and pressed the spacebar with my knuckle. The computer clicked on and there in the middle of the screen, open in a photo-editing program, was an image of an older man, who wasn't Vance, and a young girl. She couldn't have been older than five. And she was naked. She sat atop a large wooden desk in front of a regal bookcase that looked like it should be in a mansion or a museum. It was large with thick wooden rails and stiles and it was lined with books. Hardbacks. The kind with thick covers and gilded pages. The kind you buy to show off, not read.

There was a logo in the bottom right of the photo. A pitchfork with devil horns on top with the words "The Devil's Den" in a circle around it. My stomach churned at the photo and I wanted to know what it was, why Vance had it and whether it was connected to his childcare operation. I couldn't recall if I had seen this girl at the Tot Spot when I toured the place, but I couldn't shake that smoke detector in the bathroom.

A quick search of the desktop folder didn't reveal any additional photos, but that didn't mean they weren't there. I opened Vance's email program, attached the image to a new email and sent it to my encrypted account. It was a large file and I watched as the progress bar slowly filled in. I thought I heard a car pull up in front of the house, but I stayed focused on the screen in front of me. The progress bar choked past seventy-five percent. A car door slammed shut. Ninety percent. I turned and looked over my shoulder toward the front door, which was blocked by a partial wall.

A key turned in the front door lock and it swung open as the email sent. I quickly went into the email program's sent folder and deleted the record of the email. Heavy boots crossed the room on the other side of the wall as I exited the email program, closed the laptop and slipped through the door back into the garage.

I ran behind a black refrigerator that stood next to the door leading into the house. The rickety knob turned and the door slowly opened. I compressed myself against the wall behind the refrigerator. I clenched a fist, ready to hammer Vance or whoever else came into the garage. A heavy swing would lay him out and give me enough time to get out of the house. But he didn't come into the garage. Whoever it was only stood on the threshold, neither coming nor going. I slowly breathed through my mouth, careful not to make a sound.

The door finally closed and I heard the heavy footsteps move across the kitchen floor. With Vance inside the house my escape route through the basement was off the table, so I headed to the large double doors at the front of the garage to slip out, but the automatic garage door opener on the ceiling held the door closed. More footsteps pounded across the floor, faster this time, and I returned to my spot behind the refrigerator, again ready to swing if he came into the garage, but the interior door didn't open.

It neared one o'clock in the afternoon and that meant Vance still had several hours left at the daycare, so all I had to do was wait him out until he went back to work. I stayed behind the refrigerator listening to the footsteps walk through the hall beyond the door. A few minutes later I heard Vance slam the front door, start up his car on the other side of the large garage door and pull out of the driveway. I opened the interior door and walked through the kitchen.

The laptop was gone.

CHAPTER 26

THE WORLD IS full of monsters and I've come face-to-face with a lot of them, but what I saw in that photo and in Vance's basement took things to another level. I didn't like knowing what people were capable of. Most of us sleep at night because we think the world is a good place. But when you see shit like that it makes you wonder how some people get wired so differently.

When I got back to the hotel I signed into my email account to find Vance's email sitting at the top of my inbox. I forwarded the email to Cricket and dialed him.

"Whatcha need?" he said.

"Ever hear of Devil's Den?"

He thought for a moment. "It's a pile of boulders on the Gettysburg Battlefield. Took the kids there a few years ago for vacation."

"I'm not sure what surprises me more, that you have kids or that you took them to a Civil War battlefield for vacation. They were probably bored out of their minds. You're a horrible parent."

"No, I'm a history buff."

"Regardless, I'm not talking about *that* Devil's Den. Ever hear of it in reference to child pornography?"

"Fuck no. Why would I?"

"I sent you an email. Open the attachment."

He slapped a few keys on his keyboard and waited in silence. "Jesus Christ, man. You trying to get me arrested? Just having this is a federal offense. Where did you get it?"

"Never mind that. The logo on the bottom. Devil's Den. That's what I wanted to know about. It's got to be a website or something. Trades in this kind of smut."

"I'd guess so. Nothing I've ever heard of, but then again I'm not a connoisseur of child pornography. I can make a few calls and get back to you."

"Thanks. Call me as soon as you can." I clicked off the phone.

I didn't want to open the image, but I needed to see if anything in there could help me identify the piece of shit responsible for the photo. An hour ago all I wanted to do was grab my photos from Vance's house and then call in Willie's cavalry to take care of him, but I let myself get pulled into a side investigation. For some reason, I felt like I owed it to the little girl in the photo, and in some ways to Josh Baker, to see where this rabbit hole went.

My hand hovered over my laptop's trackpad, hesitating. After a deep breath I double clicked the attachment and the file opened.

As I stared at it, my eyes widened. The image turned my stomach and it made me want to punch someone in the face. Anyone.

The girl was on the left side of the photo. She sat naked atop a desk staring directly up at the camera, which shot her at a downward angle. The way she focused on the camera with a broken expression made it appear as though she was pleading for help, and I couldn't help but think she'd been in this position more times than anyone ever should. The man, who stood to the girl's left, my right, stared at the side of her face. The entire image had a strange and uncomfortable aspect to it, as if it were out of perspective or something, with him looking at her and her looking at me. I chalked that up to the subject matter and my urge to close the image as soon as possible.

I studied the man, but at first glance there wasn't anything unique about him. Nothing about his clothes stood out. No identifying marks. I turned to the bookcase and scanned it, looking for anything that offered a clue. Nothing. Then I moved to the desk. The desk was littered with papers and envelopes. It was tough to tell if it had been staged to look that way or if it was just your everyday disorganized desk. Regardless, it didn't take long to find it. In the back corner of the desk, partly obscured by a computer monitor, was a *Memphis Business Journal*. Had it not been for the slightly elevated camera, I would never have been able to see the newspaper. Dumb luck.

A feeling of disgust surged over me and I closed the photo, knowing I'd have to reopen it again later to finish examining it for any signs of the man's identity. I stood up and felt my throat tighten. I couldn't remember the last time I had such a physical response to a photograph, but I did know that I needed some fresh air before tackling the photo again.

After spending ten minutes pacing the parking lot, I returned to my room and the buzzing sound of my cell.

"I've got some information for you," said Cricket.

"That was fast."

"No, that was good." He paused. "The Devil's Den is a network for child porn, that much you already knew. But here's the rest. An earlier version of the site was called Innocent Images. It was torched by the FBI about eight months ago in a big-time sting. Lot of people got caught up in it. Seems the FBI was able to get an image onto the site and whenever someone clicked on it some file was installed on their system that let the FBI tap into their computer. They got thousands of user names and made a shit-ton of arrests. But they never got the person running it."

"How did he slip through?"

"Not sure, but the rumor is whoever was running it laid low for a while and then set up the Devil's Den as a big fuck you to law enforcement."

"Why hasn't the FBI hacked the new site? Like they did to the last one?"

"The operator learned from his past mistake. Now it's a closed network. You have to be invited to join. The customers are vetted so they can weed out any Feds. Apparently users have a secure way to upload images, but I don't know how. Since it's a closed network, there's no chance the Feds can upload a tainted file like they did before. And since the user base is much smaller, it's easier for the operator to track who is uploading images. No Feds, no malware, and no busts."

"That's fucked up."

"Of course it is," said Cricket. "Did you examine the photo? Find out who this fucktard is?"

I reluctantly reopened the photo. "I'm looking at it again now."

"Did you see it?" asked Cricket.

"The newspaper? Yeah, I saw it. It gives me a city, but not much else."

"There's more."

I could sense the ridicule in Cricket's voice and I quickly scanned the photo again to see what I'd overlooked that was so obvious. Nothing jumped out at me. "What did I miss?"

"The bookshelf. Right side, third row down. There's a book. *Dracula* by Bram Stoker."

"I know who wrote *Dracula*. What's so special about it?"

"In addition to being a history buff, I'm also a fan of rare books, and that book is as rare as a three-dicked turtle. With that edition... There's maybe five in the world, and in the right circles it's a goddamn badge of honor. Someone will know who owns it."

"*Dracula*? I've got a copy on my bookshelf. From college. How rare can it be?"

"No, you have a shitty paperback. Probably packaged with *Frankenstein* and *The Curious Case of Dr. Jekyll and Mr. Hyde*. When *Dracula* was published in 1897 the first editions were released with a yellow cloth cover. The one in the photo is still a first edition, but it has the black leather cover with gold lettering."

"I don't know what any of that means," I said.

"It means it's rare. Like worth-sixty-grand rare."

"So someone at a rare books store in Memphis would probably know where to find one."

"Now you're thinking."

I nodded and smiled. "Thanks, Cricket. I'd have never figured that out."

"Of course not. That's why you've got me. Now go get that piece of shit and have some fun doing it."

"I will. And Cricket?"

"Yeah?"

"My copy of *Dracula* did come with *Frankenstein* and Jekyll and Hyde."

"Of course it did, Finn. Of course it did." He hung up.

Cricket had always been full of surprises, but I was still shocked to learn the person I'd once paid to hack into a cell phone to get a bank president's sexting photos was also a rare book scholar.

I closed the photo on my laptop hoping I'd never have to see it again. Then I turned to my cell and searched for a rare books store in Memphis. A few seconds later a man named Anthony at the Rare Book Room answered my call.

"Hi, Anthony. Long shot here, but I'm looking for a first edition of *Dracula*. The black leather edition. You happen to have one?"

"I wish. I've got the yellow cloth, but no black edition. I think Bob Billings has one." He spoke to me like I was part of some inner circle of rare book collectors. "I don't think he's looking to sell, but you can give him a call. Want his number?"

"He local?"

"He is."

"Then, yeah, I'll take that number."

He gave me Billings's phone number and I hung up. Thanks to a literature lesson from a jack-of-all-trades criminal, the politeness of a book dealer, and a reverse phone search, I had my pedophile.

CHAPTER 27

I RAN a Tennessee DMV search and pulled up driver's license information for every Bob Billings and Robert Billings in Memphis. The searches returned nine hits. I weeded out most of the individuals from their appearance or age. That left two potential men. I opened the image I lifted from Vance and compared the driver's license photo to the Devil's Den image. Even though I only had a profile to work with on Vance's image, it was easy to make a match with the license photo. I found my mark, and thanks to the address on the license I knew where he lived.

I ran a second DMV search on Billings's address and didn't get any hits, which meant there were no other registered drivers in Memphis living at that address. I also ran his address through an online public record aggregator, which scans public sources like voter registration records, utilities information and mortgage documents and didn't find any other names linked to that address. It wasn't perfect, but I had more information telling me Billings lived alone than telling me he didn't.

I was so close to wrapping up the Vance and Tuner case, and I didn't want to get sidetracked by taking a trip to Memphis, but then a realization hit me. Killing Vance was an easy way out. Willie

Baker wanted Vance to suffer, and he probably thought the only way to make that happen was to crush his skull with a hammer. But now there was another way. Cricket said the Devil's Den was a closed network, and since Vance had that photo on his laptop he was involved somehow. If I could link him to the Devil's Den and build a case against him, I could turn the evidence over to the FBI and send him to prison, potentially for the rest of his life. And if he went to prison, it was likely his new and real identities would unravel and Willie could expose him as Josh Baker's murderer, which to me felt more like justice than simply removing him from the gene pool.

The more I thought about it, the more I looked forward to the drive to Memphis. I grabbed my .45, a to-go coffee from the Travelodge cafe and headed for the Volunteer State.

IT TOOK ME SEVEN HOURS AND A NEW APPLICATION OF DUCT TAPE TO drive from Flower Mound to Memphis. I arrived at 5711 East Tall Oaks a little after 9 p.m. and parked across the street. Billings's McMansion made Turner's high-class pad look like a fixer upper. Everything about the place screamed money, and I was no longer surprised at the idea of him having a book valued at over sixty-grand on his bookcase. Billings lived in the type of neighborhood where you wouldn't find a smashed-to-shit Lincoln Navigator parked on the side of the road. I stuck out like a dick at a funeral and could be only minutes away from some nosy neighbor calling in a suspicious vehicle.

I didn't have a lot of time, so I grabbed my .45, tucked it into my waistband and approached the house. Two panes of glass flanked the walnut front door and I could see Billings sitting on a leather sofa with a laptop across his knees. He looked like any typical fifty-year-old man with money. He was slightly balding, but had a tan that told me he'd recently been someplace sunny. He wore an ivory turtleneck and gray slacks. He didn't look like someone who made a living exploiting children, rather he looked like everyone's jolly uncle. The Devil's Den photo told me otherwise.

Billings was a monster who prayed on children who couldn't protect themselves. There's a special place in hell for people like him and I was half tempted to initiate the journey, but first I needed information. I wanted to know how Vance got the photos and what role he played in the Devil's Den operation. Since Billings was starring in his own photo shoot, which somehow found its way to Vance, I'd push him to explain the process and the players.

I hoped to temper my disgust and my fist long enough to get the information I needed, but I didn't have high hopes. I gripped my .45 in my right hand, took a step backward and drove the heel of my boot into the door just next to the brushed nickel doorknob. A perfectly aimed shot knocked the front door wide open and sent scraps of wood trim sliding across the living room floor. With the door open, I walked in with my .45 raised directly at Billings's sternum. Discretion didn't follow me into the house; it waited in the car.

As soon as I was in the foyer, Billings slammed the laptop shut and tossed it aside.

"It's encrypted, you'll never be able to access it."

When presented with a handgun to the face, most people shut down. The sight of looking down that dark tunnel tends to render most people a blabbering sack of useless shit. But it was as if Billings didn't even notice the weapon pointed at him. He was less concerned about eating a bullet and more concerned with whatever he had on that laptop. He probably thought I was law enforcement and that I was looking for evidence. That was his first mistake.

"What did you say?"

"I said it's encrypted and you can't open it. No one can. It doesn't matter if you get a warrant or not."

"I don't give two fucks about your encryption."

"No one can access it," he said. "No one."

"You can."

His forehead dripped like a fat man at a gym. "But I won't."

I closed his front door as far as I could on account of the broken doorjamb and then turned back toward him. "The error you've made is that you think I'm some sort of law enforcement officer. Your mistake should be evident by now, because if I were a cop I wouldn't be alone. There'd be a half-dozen men with me and they'd already be rifling through your shit looking for something. And you'd be facedown on the ground with your hands zip-tied behind your back. That'd probably give you a hard on."

He squinted at me.

"But I'm not here to arrest you, and as far as that laptop goes, if I want you to unlock it you will. Or I'll remove your fingers with a steak knife so the only way you'll be able to jerk off to kiddie porn again is by using your elbows."

He eyeballed the laptop but didn't say anything.

I stepped forward, rested my boot on his coffee table and leaned over toward him. "You're going to tell me about the Devil's Den. I want to know how you're involved and I want to know how Jake Polling is involved."

"I don't know who that is."

I raised my boot and slammed it into the top edge of the coffee table, sending it crashing into his shins and pinning him to the sofa. He opened his mouth to scream and I shoved the barrel of the .45 past his front teeth, knocking two of them out in the process. He clamped his bloody mouth around the barrel as tears streamed down his face.

"I'll ask again. Do you know how Jake Polling is involved?"

He slowly shook his head from side to side. His lower jaw chattered against my weapon. I withdrew it and replaced my boot on the table, keeping the sharp pressure on his shins.

"Tell me about the Devil's Den."

"It's a website. With kids on it. But I don't know who that guy is. The one you mentioned."

"How are you involved in the site?"

"I'm... just a member. That's all."

"What kind of member?"

"I pay a fee and send them pictures. And I get to see other people's photos."

I didn't say anything.

"Every member has to upload five images a month to the site," he said, wiping the blood from his mouth. "Everyone does. In addition to the monthly fee. If you don't upload the images, they cancel your membership."

"So they're crowdsourcing kiddie porn? That's sick."

He didn't respond.

I pressed harder on the table and he started to scream but I shoved the .45 back in his face. He covered his mouth with both hands, his eyes still watering.

"What else do you know about it? Who runs it?"

He removed his hands from his mouth. "I don't remember his name."

"You sure it's not Jake Polling? Think real hard."

He shook his head. "No. Not Polling. I don't know who that is. It's... Vincent... Vince..."

It hadn't dawned on me until then that maybe Vance wasn't going by Polling while working with the Devil's Den. He'd want to protect the Jake Polling identity. Keep it clean. Maybe he used his real name to distance himself from the operation. His real identity would be scrubbed clean and there was no link to Jake Polling. Few people outside of Parkersburg, West Virginia, would know who Jacob Vance was, so it made sense.

"You mean Vance? Jacob Vance?"

Billings snapped his head up as if something clicked inside. "Yes, Vance. But no... wait, not Jacob." He wiped his face. "Thomas Vance. Yeah, Tom Vance."

"Thomas Vance?"

He nodded his head.

That was a name I hadn't expected to hear. But now Nell's theory about Thomas using his government connections to weasel his son into federal protection started looking like a solid bet. Cricket mentioned the Feds taking down a child pornography network, but weren't able to snare the operator. Could Thomas be using his connections to stay one step ahead? To stay insulated and protected? It fit, but I wanted to know more about the operation.

"How do you upload your photos?" I asked. "Where do you send them?"

"I have a thumb drive." He pointed to the laptop next to him. There was a yellow thumb drive with the Devil's Den logo plugged into the laptop's USB port. "I upload them and someone on the other ends stamps a watermark on it and then uploads it to the site for everyone to see."

I thought back to what Cricket said about a secure means to upload images.

"Give me the thumb drive," I said.

"I can't do that."

I grabbed Billings's turtleneck and yanked him forward. His legs were still wedged between the sofa and the hard edges of the coffee table. As I jerked him forward, he placed his hands on the coffee table to brace himself. That's when I slammed the butt of my .45 down on his left index and middle fingers. The bones shattered between my weapon and the wooden table. It sounded like I'd just stepped on a dozen cockroaches. He screamed and I slammed the butt into the side of his open jaw, which knocked him sideways on the sofa, but his pinned legs held his bottom half upright.

Hitting Billings felt good, almost too good. The kind of good that if you don't pull back you could go too far.

"Sure you can," I said.

Billings's face looked like a car window in a thunderstorm. He righted himself and plucked the thumb drive from the laptop with his good hand. My eyes wandered to his left hand. His fingers had already begun to swell, and while there was no other visible trauma I knew I'd turned the bones to peanut brittle. He handed the thumb drive to me and began gasping for air, his mouth open wide.

"I can't breathe," he said.

"Yes you can. You're just hyperventilating."

"No, I can't breathe."

"You're talking, so you're breathing. Slow your breaths, because I need you conscious."

Billings stared up at me like an animal in a snare. His expression looked familiar. Like the one the little girl wore in the photo I'd found on Vance's computer.

"What about the girl in your photo?"

"Which photo?"

It didn't hit me until then that there were more. Probably a lot more. Too many for him to know whom I was talking about. "The one with the girl sitting on a desk. She couldn't have been more than five. There was a bookcase in the background. A real big one. That clear it up?"

He thought for a moment. "That was a long time ago. I don't remember her name."

My fingers tightened around my .45 and I had to stop myself from hitting him again. It wasn't an easy decision to make.

"Here's what's going to happen," I said, slipping the thumb drive into my pocket. "The Devil's Den is going to get shit-canned, and so is Thomas Vance."

He nodded.

"And sometime soon, the police are going to come knocking on your door. They'll arrest you and you're going to tell them everything you know about the operation. Then they'll charge you and you'll plead guilty. There won't be a trial and you'll probably spend the rest of your life in prison."

He buried his face in his hands again.

"I'll be looking in on you, Bob. And if it goes down any other way, I'll come back here and torture you, and then I'll murder you. And I promise you won't see me coming."

He rolled over onto his side, still gasping for air.

I tucked the .45 into my waistband, returned to my car and drove back to Texas.

CHAPTER 28

I RETURNED to my hotel in Flower Mound close to five in the morning. I was asleep before my head hit the pillow. Josh Baker visited me again that night in my dreams. This time he brought my daughter, Becca. The lush green field was gone. Instead Josh ran across a playground with my daughter chasing him, her arms open wide in an exaggerated attempt to catch him. The playground looked like the place where I first met Willie Baker in Parkersburg weeks ago. I watched as Becca chased Josh up the slide and then across to the swings. When she finally caught him she wrapped her outstretched arms around him, lifted him off the ground and twirled him around. She set him down and turned to me, as if she had just realized I was there.

She ran toward me, her arms open wide again. I knelt down and opened my own arms to catch her, but she stopped before she reached me. She turned to see someone else walking out of the woods that bordered the back of the playground. It was Jacob Vance. I yelled to her to come to me, but she didn't hear me. She walked toward Vance, who stood at the tree line beckoning her forward. I wanted to run to her and grab her, but I couldn't move. Only watch as she stepped closer and closer to him. A moment later

Josh Baker was next to her. He took hold of her right hand with his left and they walked toward the woods together. I screamed for them to stop, to get away from Vance, but they ignored me. All I could do was watch as they reached him. He stepped aside and ushered them into the woods before turning to nod at me, and then disappeared into the tree line behind them.

I woke up pounding the sheets. It was 8:30 in the morning.

I didn't want Vance dead. I wanted him to rot in prison. That meant collecting all the evidence I could and turning it over to the FBI to shut him down. According to Cricket, the Feds had already killed the website's previous incarnation and they'd jump at the chance to try again. I had the thumb drive, but I needed Vance's laptop to bring down the Devil's Den and Jacob and Thomas Vance with it.

I rolled out of bed, headed for the parking lot and made it to Vance's home by nine. His SUV wasn't in the driveway and he should be at the childcare center. I parked in the same spot I'd parked two days earlier and went to work.

Sycamore Street was deserted except for a silver sedan and SUV and a black pickup truck. Seeing the SUV made me think about the one that followed me near my hotel. I convinced myself that it was a coincidence and that if I looked hard enough I'd see silver SUVs everywhere. I shook off the paranoia and moved on.

I slipped on my gloves and entered Vance's home through the cellar door. I moved through the kitchen and into the living room. That's where I nearly tripped over him. There, in the middle of the floor, was Jacob Vance. He was lying in a pool of blood that still seeped from a fist-sized hole in the side of his head. Next to him on the floor was a claw hammer.

The overturned coffee table and shattered wall mirror told me that Vance didn't go down quietly, and with the houses so close together it was likely a neighbor heard the struggle and called the police. I couldn't take a chance on being there when they showed up. As I turned to leave the room, I saw the laptop on the carpet propped up against the sofa.

I grabbed it, made my way back through the basement and climbed out from under the cellar door. After realigning the hinge screws over their holes and stomping them back into place, I headed for my car. The first thing I noticed was that my legs moved faster than they had on the way to Vance's house. The second thing I noticed was that the silver SUV was gone.

When I turned the corner onto the street where I parked, I saw someone sitting on the hood of my Navigator. From a distance I couldn't identify him. He wore a black jacket, gray slacks and black dress shoes. As I got closer I noticed it wasn't a black jacket. It was a black sweater. A turtleneck sweater. That and the neatly parted gray hair gave him away. Little Freddie.

I'd worked with Little Freddie two years ago while trying to find a blackmailer for an underground information broker in Ohio. Little Freddie was the worst kind of killer. After a mob butcher snuffed out his wife and daughter he had nothing left to lose, and that made him more dangerous than a man with sweaty palms juggling live hand grenades.

During our last case together, Little Freddie tortured a police informant with a steel baton and a pair of pliers, dismembered a mob lieutenant in an Indiana cornfield, and murdered the man who'd hired us. He was the perfect person to kill Vance.

"Christ, kid," he said, flicking a cigarette onto the sidewalk. "You can actually drive in this piece of shit?"

"When I left Cincinnati it was in one piece. You're not helping things by sitting on it."

He stood up. "Good to see you again, Finn. How's things?"

"Things were cream and caramels until about ten minutes ago." I looked beyond Freddie and noticed the silver SUV parked in front of my wounded Navigator had Texas plates.

"How long you been on my ass?" I asked.

"Since Parkersburg."

"Bullshit."

"You're not the only one on Willie Baker's payroll. You were phase one. I'm phase two."

"That's one hell of a coincidence, him finding both of us."

"He didn't find you. He found me, but I knew I'd never be able to locate these two asshats so I told him I knew someone who could. You. The way I see it, you owe me a referral fee."

"That's not how Willie sold it to me."

"We thought it best to leave me out of it," he said. "Didn't want to influence your decision to take the case. I figured you'd say no if you knew I was involved."

"I would have."

"And there aren't many other people who could find Vance and Turner, so I guess we made the right decision." He put his arm around my shoulder. "Though I guess you can go on home now. You finished your job. Now I need to go finish mine."

I shook my head. "Turner lives."

"Bullshit he does. He murdered a kid, Finn. And you know how that sits with me."

"He lives," I said. "I met him the other day. Looked him right in the eye. Talked to him. He's turned his life around. He's helping people. Probably as a means to pay for what he did to Willie's son. There's no need to kill him."

"I don't care if he's giving Easter baskets to orphans. He killed that boy in West Virginia, and that's all the convincing I need."

"He'll do more good alive."

"That's the difference between me and you. You like to rationalize things. Weigh the consequences. Me? I just don't give a fuck." Little Freddie walked toward the silver SUV. "He'd already be dead had you not dragged my ass all the way to Memphis."

"You followed me there?"

"And back. Didn't expect you to return to Vance's place."

"Plans change."

"Mine hasn't." Little Freddie opened his driver door and bent down low, as if reaching under the seat, and then stood. "Now it's time for you to go home, Finn. Get back in that piece of shit and pray it holds together long enough to get you back to Cincinnati. Where it's safe."

"Turner lives."

"No. He don't." Freddie pulled a suppressed 9mm from his SUV and raised it chest level. "Go home, Finn. Get in that car and drive away now or I'll shoot you in the gut and disappear before anyone even notices you're dying on the sidewalk."

I didn't have a choice. I wasn't going to convince Freddie to let Turner go and there wasn't much else I could do standing on the street with a weapon in my face.

"You're making a mistake," I said.

"It ain't the first or the last, kid."

I stepped into my car, set the laptop on the backseat, fired the engine and pulled away from the curb. My gut told me Freddie would head straight for Turner. There was no reason to wait. Once the word got out that Vance was dead, Valerie would relocate Turner, or at least throw some protection his way. Freddie knew that too, so he'd move fast. Had Turner not convinced me otherwise, I would have pointed my car toward Cincinnati and never looked back, but he didn't deserve to die. In eighty-four he was a gullible kid who blindly followed Vance in some sick pursuit. Josh Baker got a raw deal and Vance paid for it. Turner didn't have to.

As I watched Little Freddie waving to me in the rearview mirror, I reached for my phone in the console to call Turner, but the phone was gone. Freddie must have yanked it before I got back to the car. All he had to do was reach through the tarp-covered window.

I couldn't risk stopping to find a pay phone. Little Freddie was probably already moving. I had to warn Turner in person.

CHAPTER 29

I KEYED the address to the Raymond Asher Foundation into my GPS. The first time I went to Dallas I drove straight to Turner's home on Molly Court, but I'd get to Dallas around 10 a.m. so I had to snatch him at his office.

The corner of the tarp covering my passenger window came loose and flapped violently as I crisscrossed through traffic on SH 114 east. I shifted my eyes from the cars in front of me to my rearview mirror watching for Freddie's silver SUV. I didn't know if he thought I'd heed his advice and go back to Cincinnati, but I figured he'd move fast anyway. I thought back to Vance's body on his living room floor. Had a neighbor heard the struggle and called the police, it wouldn't take long for the dominoes to fall. The news of Vance's murder would reach Valerie's desk, and knowing I was in town actively looking for both Vance and Turner she'd pick up the phone and dial a herd of cowboy hat-adorned marshals to protect Turner. Maybe they'd get to Turner before Freddie and gun Freddie down in the parking lot before he got inside Turner's office door. But reality told me it would take time for Valerie to even get word of Vance's death. The local police didn't know Vance was in WITSEC, and unless Valerie was actively listening to a police scanner how would she know they found him?

I knew if anyone was going to get between Turner and Freddie it had to be me. I buried the accelerator and tore down the highway like a woman in labor was screaming in my passenger seat. I was watching the rearview mirror waiting for Freddie's silver grille to emerge behind me and almost clipped the back of an 18-wheeler as it swerved around a red minivan.

The duct tape on the bottom of my makeshift window finally gave way and the tarp flapped wildly against the inside of the car. A gust of air surged into the vehicle and I had to crack the driver's window to equalize the pressure pounding my ears.

I stayed ahead of Freddie for most of the 30 miles between Flower Mound and Dallas, but he caught me where SH 114 east merged into I-35E. The silver SUV closed fast in my mirror. He came up behind me, almost plowed into my bumper, and swerved into the right lane to pull alongside me. I glanced over to see him shaking his head and holding up my cell phone. He tossed it into the back of his vehicle and slammed on the gas, leaving me trapped behind a dump truck and a Prius.

I weaved through the vehicles lining up to keep me from catching Little Freddie. As he pulled farther away I saw the prospect of beating him to Turner fading away too. Maybe Freddie would go to Turner's home and I'd have time to get to his office first. No, Freddie was a professional and he'd have Turner's work schedule figured out. He'd know where to find him.

More doubt crept in as a lane of traffic opened up. I jerked the wheel to the left and pushed the accelerator to the floorboard. The Navigator lurched forward and closed on Little Freddie. My GPS chirped telling me to take Exit 423. I'd almost reached Freddie when he cut across two lanes of traffic and took Exit 424 for Illinois Avenue. My exit was a mile farther up the highway. If my route was the quickest, I still had a chance to beat Freddie to Turner's office.

I pulled off the exit and two right turns later I arrived at the strip mall. No silver SUV. Remembering the back door in Turner's office, I drove through the parking lot, pulled around the row of buildings onto the access road and stopped at the brown metal door.

My engine still hummed as I pounded on the door. Nothing. I beat on it again and this time Turner’s voice came through.

"Yes?" he said.

"Mr. Asher, this is Roger Mathers." I tried to sound like I wasn't hyperventilating. "Can you let me in?"

A dead bolt slid across the metal and Turner heaved the heavy door open.

"Hello again." He wore a concerned smile. "We have a front door—"

"Is anyone else in the office?" I interrupted.

He stepped backward. "No. They won't get in until noon." His smile disappeared. "What's going on?"

"I need you to come with me." I reached for his arm but he yanked it away.

"What are you talking about? I'm not going anywhere."

"We don't have a lot of time. I'm not here to learn about your charity. Willie Baker hired me to find you."

Turner's eyes widened and he stumbled back, reaching his arm out for his desk chair.

"Josh Baker's father?"

"We need to move. He's only a few minutes behind me."

"Who? Willie?"

"No, the man he hired to kill you."

"What are you talking about?"

The front door chimed as Little Freddie's knees broke the infrared sensor. He saw me and charged toward the back. I grabbed Turner, jerked him from his office chair and pulled him out the door and onto the service road.

"Get in the car and I'll explain later." I opened the passenger door and pushed him into the SUV. I ran around the front of the car and climbed through the driver's door as Turner's office door flew open. We pulled away as two slugs tore through the blue tarp and cracked the windshield directly below the rearview mirror. I looked up and for the second time that morning I watched Little Freddie fade away in the rearview mirror.

"Do you have a phone on you?" I asked.

Turner yanked a phone from his pocket and held it out to me. I grabbed my wallet from my back pocket, slipped the white business card from inside and handed it to him.

"Are you going to tell me what in the shit is going on?"

"Call that number and put it on speaker."

A moment later Valerie Cheatham's voice filled the vehicle.

"This is Finn Harding. I've got Raymond Turner in my car, but he's in trouble."

"What in the hell are—"

"Someone just fired two shots at him. He's safe, but I need to bring him to you. Where's your office?"

"Dallas. 1100 Commerce Street. The federal building. How quickly can you get him here?"

"We're on our way." I snatched the phone from Turner's hand and clicked it off.

"I'm not going anywhere without Eva and Ella," said Turner. "My daughters."

Little Freddie had a knack for seeing things through, and I knew me whisking Turner away wouldn't be the end of this. Freddie would look for leverage. Something to use to get to Turner. And his girls made perfect targets.

"They're in school?" I said.

"Adelle Lee. It's on South Polk."

I glanced from the road to the phone and searched the call history for Valerie's number.

"What are you doing?"

"Calling the marshal back," I said. "I'll send her to the school."

"No." He grabbed the phone and tossed it onto the console. "I'm not risking a shootout at my kid's school. We can get there quicker."

I looked at the two bullet holes in my windshield. "Okay. How do I get there?"

Turner guided me to the elementary school and I pulled into the parking lot. My Navigator slammed into a yellow speed bump, which jarred the vehicle, and I waited for my bumper to break free, but somehow it hung on. I stopped in the fire lane in front of the main entrance and Turner reached for the door handle.

"Your first instinct might be to grab those girls and run, but don't," I said. "I can get you to the marshal's office. And that's the safest place right now."

"And my wife, Christina," he said. "I'll call her as soon as I get the girls and have her meet us there."

I handed him the phone. "Call her on your way in."

Turner pushed open the door and climbed out. As he walked through the main entrance I grabbed the .45 from my bag and scanned the parking lot for Little Freddie's SUV. Nothing. After a few minutes, I leaned back to check the main entrance through the rear passenger window, but no girls and no Turner. I looked through the windshield and saw a silver SUV pull into the far entrance and stop in the middle of the parking lot. There was no license plate on the front bumper and it was too far away to see if Freddie was behind the wheel. It rolled forward a few feet and stopped.

My fingers tensed around my weapon. The SUV rolled forward a few more feet and then stopped again. I watched the SUV sit in the same spot for ten minutes. The sound of girls laughing trickled through the two small holes in the blue tarp and I leaned back to see Turner, Ella and Eva approach the rear of the car. As they climbed into the back seat, the silver SUV rolled forward.

What if he rams me? Or opens fire on the entire vehicle?

Gunning for Turner was one thing, but now I had two girls in the backseat.

"Come on, hurry up," I said. Turner clicked the seatbelts around his daughters and climbed in between them. I pulled away from the curb before Turner had a chance to close the back door. As he reached for the door the silver SUV picked up speed and headed for us. I clenched the leather steering wheel with my left hand and raised the .45 with my right.

"Get down," I said to the backseat.

Turner put one arm around each daughter and leaned them as forward as they could go with the seatbelts around them.

As the silver SUV crept past us, I saw a woman talking on a cell phone behind the wheel.

Once we passed, I set my weapon on the passenger seat and gave Turner the all clear. He, Eva and Ella sat up in the backseat.

"Daddy, where are we going?"

"We're going to get mommy," said Turner.

"What?" I said. "I thought you told her to meet us at the marshal's office."

"I forgot about her car. It's at the dealer. It was recalled."

"How did you forget that?"

"It's a little tough to concentrate with all this going on. I've been driving her to work. She's going to meet us in the lobby." He paused. "I didn't tell her why."

"Okay, how do I get to her office?"

Turner was giving me directions when his cell rang. He answered it and then handed it to me.

"He wants to talk to you," he said.

"Hello, Finn," said Little Freddie.

"How'd you get this number?"

"It's on the brochure I took from Turner's office." He paused. "You went for the kids didn't you?"

"Yeah," I said.

"Figured. I went for the wife. Wanna trade?"

"Not really."

"I don't have to tell you what happens if you don't."

"What is it?" asked Turner. "Is Christina okay?"

"Tell him she's fine," said Little Freddie, hearing Turner through the phone. "Whether she stays that way is completely up to him." He paused. "There's a park about a mile from her office. The one with the giant blue dinosaur slide. I'll assume Turner knows where it is. You've got twenty minutes to get there. I'll swap the wife for Turner."

I didn't say anything.

"And Finn, don't fuck this up."

I clicked off the phone. Turner leaned forward wedging himself between the two front seats.

"What did he say? Is Christina all right?"

"She’s fine, but he wants to trade her for you."

Turner was quiet for a moment. "Then do it."

I lowered my voice so the girls in the backseat didn't hear me. "If you get out of this car, he'll shoot you dead on the spot. That's his job."

"I don't care. I'm not risking her life for mine." He dropped his face into his hands. "Where are they?"

"Some park with a dinosaur slide. Near her office. You know it?"

"Red Oak Park. We have lunch there sometimes."

I clicked on Turner's phone, scrolled through the recent calls, found Valerie's number and dialed.

"What is it now?" she said, recognizing the number.

"We've got a problem," I said, pressing the phone tight against my ear. "How quickly can you get to Red Oak Park?"

"Why?"

"I've got Turner and his daughters in my car, but they've got his wife at the park. They want to trade her for Turner."

"Jesus Christ. Could you fuck things up any worse?"

"Look, I'm trying to help. Can you get to the park?"

"Where is it?"

I looked at Turner. "Where's the park?"

"It's near the golf course where 342 and 77 connect," said Turner.

I repeated the directions to Valerie.

She was quiet for a moment. "I'll get there, but you've got to stall them. It's going to take me some time."

"Okay," I said. "You might want to be discrete. They suspect anything and she's dead."

"You want to lecture me about being discreet? Your discretion got us in this clusterfuck in the first place. I told you to stay the fuck out of it and look what happened."

"You're wasting time. Just get to the park. I'll stall as long as I can."

"Stay out of our way when we get there." She hung up.

I handed the phone back to Turner.

"Did you find Jacob?" he asked.

"I found him. He was living in Flower Mound."

"Here in Texas? Why so close? I figured he'd be on the other side of the country."

"You both had the same handler. The marshal we just spoke with. Guess she wanted to keep you close."

"I don't remember speaking to any marshals."

"Guess she was behind the scenes. Dallas is a big city. She could keep an eye on both of you and there was little chance you two would bump into each other."

"I wouldn't even know what he looks like." He paused. "What was his name? Since going under?"

"Jake Polling. He ran a daycare."

"You met him?"

"Yes.

"Did you tell him about Josh's father too?"

I didn't answer, but Turner interpreted my silence for what it was.

"He's dead isn't he?"

"Yeah. He is."

"Why didn't you give me up then?"

"At first, I was going to." I lowered my voice again. "But then I saw what you'd become, what you did to help those kids, and I didn't think you needed your skull crushed with a hammer. The day you showed me those photos in your office, that's when I decided I wasn't going to throw you to the wolves. I'm not saying it makes up for what you did to Josh Baker, but I guess it's worth a reprieve."

"Who is Josh?" asked one of his daughters.

"Someone daddy knew a long time ago," he said.

"I hope that haunts you forever," I said.

"It's why I get out of bed every morning."

He exhaled a deep breath, leaned back in the seat and guided me to the park.

CHAPTER 30

WE ARRIVED at Red Oak Park a few minutes before Little Freddie's deadline. Children littered the playground. They climbed on the giant dinosaur, kicked balls in an open field and dashed beneath several large oak trees that formed a long tunnel in the field.

Little Freddie's silver SUV was at the far end of the parking lot. It backed up against a steep berm that formed the rear boundary of the park.

I pulled to a stop about one hundred yards from the SUV. I scanned the park grounds looking for Valerie or anyone who might be working with her. Nothing. I watched in the rearview mirror as Turner hugged his daughters and whispered something into their ears, but I couldn't make it out. He glanced up at me.

"What are we supposed to do now?" he asked.

"Sit here for a long as we can and hope the marshal comes through."

The phone rang.

"Tell him to walk over to my car," said Freddie. "I let his wife walk as soon as he gets here."

I stepped outside the SUV so the girls wouldn't hear me. "I've got Turner's daughters in the backseat. How do I know you won't off him and his wife?"

"I have no interest in orphaning those kids, Finn. The wife walks as soon as Turner steps to the car. You've got my word."

I checked my watch. "Okay, but give the guy a few minutes. He knows it's the last time he'll see his kids."

"He's got two minutes. That's it."

I hung up the phone and scanned the parking lot again. No Valerie. No team. No cowboy hats.

Goddamn it. Where are you?

Two minutes passed and the phone rang.

"Now!" said Little Freddie.

Turner opened the rear car door and hugged his daughters again. I didn't know what he said to them, but it was obvious they had no idea what was happening. He peered at me but didn't say anything. He didn't have to. I'd seen that expression before. He looked like a man who knew he was about to die.

"All right," I said, then hung up the phone.

Turner closed the door and I stared at him over the roof.

"Walk slow. Real slow."

TURNER WAS HALFWAY TO THE SILVER SUV WHEN THE FIRST marshal came over the berm. Within seconds four others, including Valerie, had surrounded the car. One approached the driver's door with his weapon raised. He yelled something, but I couldn't make it out. A moment later he fired four bursts through the driver's window. At the same time, someone on the other side of the SUV yanked the rear door open with one hand while training a weapon in the backseat with the other. He pulled a woman, who I assumed was Turner's wife, out of the vehicle as Valerie looked on a few feet away. The marshal who had fired at Little Freddie gave an all-clear signal and the remaining marshals holstered their firearms and helped Christina off the ground. It was over in less than ten seconds.

Turner sprinted across the parking lot and wrapped his arms around his wife. Valerie walked to him, patted Turner on the shoulder and waved me over.

The marshals cleared the playground of people as I slowly drove over to the silver SUV.

"Get out of the car," said Valerie. She didn't have to repeat herself. She pointed to the SUV. "Do you know who that was?"

"No."

"No? All this bullshit and you don't even know who you were up against?"

"Like I said, I was hired to find him. That's all."

"By whom?"

I didn't say anything.

"I'll spare your conscience and just assume it was Willie Baker." She squinted at me. "What am I going to find when I leave here and go to Flower Mound?"

"Nothing good," I said.

"And you had nothing to do with it? I find that hard to believe."

"It's the truth. I was hired to find Vance and Turner. Nothing more." I pointed to the silver SUV. "I didn't know he was following me."

"So you led him right to them?"

"I guess so."

"You must have been a really shitty PI." She shook her head. "Don't think you're walking away from this unscathed. I'm still holding you responsible. There *will* be an investigation."

"One thing your investigator might want to look into is the video camera tucked inside the smoke detector in the boys' bathroom at Vance's daycare center. I'd check the girls' bathroom too. Check his computer and you'll probably find what he's been recording. Oh, and there's this." I opened the rear door of my car and sensed Valerie's hand go to her hip. She relaxed when the two girls jumped out and ran to their parents.

I handed Valerie Vance's laptop and the yellow USB drive from Memphis.

"What's this?"

"Vance was involved in some child porn ring. Your friends in the FBI will cream their Men's Wearhouse slacks when you turn this over. Apparently they've been looking for the guy behind this operation for a long time. This will help them find him. In Parkersburg."

She smirked.

"Oh, and have fun explaining why someone under your protection was shooting and distributing child pornography under your nose. That won't look too good."

"Technically Vance was no longer under my watch. He opted out of protection ten years ago. I checked in on him from time to time as a favor to my boss, but he wasn't my responsibility."

"But Turner was?"

"Turner was terrified someone would come after him. He followed every rule we gave him. Television stations hounded him for interviews about the missing kids his organization helped find, but he refused every one because he didn't want his face out there. He really tried to do it right. Turned his life around. I like to think he started the charity to make up for the Baker kid." She stopped herself. "To make up for what he did to Josh."

A black minivan with blue-and-white government license plates parked next to my SUV. Two men in blue-and-yellow US Marshal jackets stepped out of the back, ushered Turner, his wife and two daughters into the van and drove away.

"I think Turner did all right given his past," I said. "But how did the Feds get roped into protecting him and Vance anyway? Doesn't seem like a good use of taxpayer resources."

"Of course it isn't a good use of resources. I don't know how it happened. That was all before my time. I just lucked into the detail.

And by luck I mean got shit on. But thanks to your shitty PI work, I can put all this behind me."

"What do you mean?"

"The Marshals will relocate Turner and his family. Far away from here. It's protocol. But I'll stay put. He can be someone else's problem and I can get back to more important things, like protecting people who really deserve it." She shook her head. "I'm with you on this one. They should never have gotten the protection, but they did. And somehow I ended up running it." She poked me in the chest with a bright red fingernail. "I can't make up my mind about you."

"How's that?"

"Can't tell if those are angels or demons on your shoulder."

"Don't we all have a few of each?"

She shrugged.

"Speaking of demons, did you order a bag over my head?"

She smiled. "I don't know what you're talking about."

An ambulance pulled into the park, its red lights flashing to the wide eyes of the crowd gathered around the perimeter of the park.

"I think we're done here," she said. "Go back to Ohio. Hug that little girl of yours."

"So what about that investigation?"

"I wouldn't be too worried about that."

I nodded and turned toward my car. As I passed the silver SUV I looked through the open driver's door. There, slumped across the front seat was a thirty-something, bald, white male with four holes in his chest and what looked like a Glock in his right hand.

It wasn't Little Freddie.

CHAPTER 31

I COULDN'T WAIT to get out of Dallas. I checked out of the Travelodge in Flower Mound over the telephone and hit I-30 east twenty minutes after leaving Valerie Cheatham in Red Oak Park. I drove until sleep wouldn't let me go any farther and pulled into a rest stop north of Nashville around 11 p.m. that night. I fell asleep before I could even get my seatbelt off. I hoped Josh Baker would visit me in my dreams again, but he had something more important to do. A semi popped its airbrakes behind me and the hiss nearly sent me through the window. When I woke up, all I could think about was Becca.

Vance and Turner snuffed Josh Baker from this world in the blink of an eye. Josh's mother turned her back for a moment and countless lives changed. Josh Baker lost his life, the Bakers lost their son, Vance and Turner lost their minds, and a town lost its innocence. I'd never know why Vance and Turner did what they did. I'd never know why they picked that day, that mall or that little boy. But that's how evil works. That's how monsters live.

I made up my mind before I had a chance to wipe the drool from the side of my mouth. Becca was too important to me to let anything happen to her. I knew I couldn't protect her forever and that one day she would be somewhere my watchful eyes couldn't reach. But until then I could do everything I could do to make sure any monsters that crossed her path kept on walking. Willie Baker wanted vengeance for the ultimate loss. I wanted to never know what that felt like.

FIVE HOURS LATER I PULLED INTO MY APARTMENT BUILDING'S parking lot. Albert was watching television when I walked into our apartment. He jumped me like a swarm of mosquitos.

"You back for good this time?" he asked, wrapping an arm around me.

"I think so."

He nodded. "You know, that beard is kind of growing on me. I think I like it."

"You shitting me?"

He smiled. "Of course I'm shitting you. It looks terrible." He moved a hand across my back, as if checking for bullet holes or knife wounds. I jerked my arm to the side when he brushed my right collarbone.

"War wound?"

"Aluminum baseball bat."

"Been there."

I knew he wasn't joking.

"How was Texas?"

"I'd rather not talk about it." I saw the disappointment in his face. "Maybe later."

He walked back to the sofa, sat down and smacked the spot next to him. "Have a seat, son. Unless you got something else to do."

"Can't think of anything."

Albert clicked the remote and Jack Klugman came to life on the screen.

I sat down. "What happened to *Columbo*?"

"Finished the series. On to *Quincy* now." He looked over to me. "You should have been a doctor."

"He's not a doctor, he's a medical examiner. There's a difference, Dad."

He laughed. "I'm glad you made it back in time for Dewey's tonight," he said without taking his eyes off the screen. "Becca kept asking if you'd be there."

"Wouldn't miss it." I hadn't even realized it was Friday. "Brooke joining us again?"

"She is if you want her to."

"I'd like that." I crossed my legs. "You have any problem with her still being here in the morning?"

He shook his head and turned up the volume.

CHAPTER 32

Two weeks later I found myself drinking Yirgacheffe coffee and eating a banana nut muffin at Winans Coffee on the corner of Eighth and Walnut in downtown Cincinnati. As I sipped from my paper cup I thought about Ray Turner and wondered what city he called home now. I wondered what would become of the Asher Foundation, all the people who volunteered there, and the good work they did. Would Turner set up a new organization in his new town under his new name? I hoped his unrelenting passion to overcome what he did in Parkersburg so long ago still motivated him to get children out of the shitty situations they fell into. Maybe in the end it would all even out for him.

I was wiping the muffin crumbs from the dark brown table when I heard a familiar voice.

"Thought I'd find you here."

"I thought I'd find you peppered with bullet holes behind that SUV steering wheel."

"Hired help. I know when to handle things from a distance."

"He the kind of hired help someone is going to miss? Start asking questions about?"

"Nope."

I kicked a chair out and Little Freddie sat down. He placed a newspaper under his arm and set my cell phone and a piece of paper on the table.

"Thanks. I was beginning to think I'd have to get a new one." I turned the piece of paper over. It was a cashier's check for $100,000.

"Willie Baker paid me up front. That's your fee for finding Vance. I'm not paying you for Turner because I never got a chance to put a hammer through his skull."

I folded the check and slipped it inside my pocket. "I don't usually accept checks," I said.

"Sorry, it's all I got. It's secure."

I curled the muffin wrapper between my thumb and index finger and tossed it into a nearby garbage can. "I feel bad taking Willie's money. Figure he needs it more than me. Especially if he has to mount a legal defense."

"Don't let the prison guard uniform fool you. He's got plenty of money. He cashed out big when his wife died. A lot of zeros on her life insurance policy check. And I wouldn't worry about the law coming after him."

"It's not him I'm worried about. If they start asking questions he could lead them to me."

"He isn't going to implicate you. Besides, you didn't do anything illegal. Technically the only crime you committed was endangering the lives of everyone on the highway by driving around in that piece of shit you call a car. I saw it in the lot. You're still a bumper short."

"Haven't gotten around to fixing it yet. How do you know they won't come looking for you? To link you to Vance or Turner?"

"Because I covered my tracks on Vance and they already got the guy who went after Turner. Shot him dead in a rented SUV. You saw it." He paused. "Course if you said something about me, I don't know, maybe to your marshal friend, that could cause some problems for me."

"Never came up."

"Why not?"

I took a sip of my lukewarm coffee and leaned forward. "Because I guess we both wanted the same thing. Justice for a kid who never got to grow up. Besides, I'd rather you owe me a favor for not ratting you out than have to look over my shoulder all the time for turning you in."

"Speaking of justice, I've got something else for you." He handed me the newspaper.

"What's this?"

"Just give it a read."

I scanned the page.

Former Council Member Indicted in Child Pornography Ring

Parkersburg—Thomas Vance, 64, is facing felony charges for manufacturing and possessing child pornography after federal agents raided his home as part of an ongoing investigation.

Investigators say Vance was the leader of a sophisticated operation that trafficked illicit images of minors, some as young as five years old.

The investigation began when authorities received evidence that led to the arrest of Robert Billings, 53, of Memphis. Billings led authorities to Vance.

As a result of the raid on Vance's Parkersburg home, investigators found thousands of images of minors in sexually explicit poses, as well as hundreds of explicit videos.

Investigators also found information on more than 700 accounts to the "Devil's Den" website, a private network where users traded sexually explicit images and videos. Authorities are analyzing that information in hopes of identifying the website members, which could lead to even more arrests.

In an interesting twist, authorities also implicated Jacob Vance, 41, Thomas Vance's son, in the ring. Jacob Vance, along with Raymond Turner, was found guilty of murdering four-year-old Josh Baker in 1984. Jacob Vance had been living in Flower Mound, Texas, under the name Jacob Polling.

Polling was recently found murdered in what investigators believe was a home invasion, but do not suspect any connection between his murder and his role in the child pornography ring. That investigation is still ongoing.

Thomas Vance served as a council member in Parkersburg in the early 1980s before joining the United States Attorney's Office for the Southern District of West Virginia and then the Department of Justice in Washington, D.C. He returned to Parkersburg when he retired four years ago.

If convicted, Thomas Vance faces up to 50 years in prison.

- Nell Richards, Special to the Parkersburg Sentinel

I tossed the newspaper back to Little Freddie. "Hope it sticks," I said. "Figured you'd be pissed that I fucked up your hit on Turner. That you didn't get him."

"Just because I didn't get to him in Dallas doesn't mean I won't get him somewhere else."

"You won't have my help. I'm out." I yanked the envelope Valerie had given me from my jacket pocket. "This is my ticket out of the shadows. The Marshals reinstated my PI license."

"And why in the hell would you want to go back to that shitty work?"

"Because it's easier on the nerves. Since taking my practice underground I've been smacked around and shot at more times that I can count." I swirled the paper cup in my hand. "Thanks for shooting at me by the way. Back at the strip mall."

"I wasn't aiming for you." He smiled. "And that shitty blue tarp saved Turner's life. I'd have plugged him had I been able to see him."

"Point is, I kinda like breathing, so maybe doing corporate PI work or chasing down cheating spouses or workers comp cheats is a wiser career move. Beats looking behind you all the time watching for monsters. Or rotting away in prison for associating with the likes of you."

"You think that envelope is going to make your world a safer place? Keep the monsters at bay? Nothing is going to change that. Evil is all around us. The difference between people like us and the rest of the world? We can see it." He pointed around the room. "They can't."

I didn't say anything.

Little Freddie stood up. "Suit yourself, Finn. Seems like a boring existence to me. Either way, I'll see you around." With that he winked, turned and walked out of the coffee shop.

I was about to head to the counter for a refill when my phone buzzed on the table.

"Is this Roger Mathers?"

"Yes, it is. Who's this?"

"Nell Richards. From Parkersburg."

"Hi Nell. I just read your article on Thomas Vance. Glad to see he's on his way down."

"Me too. I'll be following that one closely. I found something you might be interested in. For your book research."

"Whatcha got?"

"So after talking to you, I went back to the *Sentinel* offices. Into the archives. I found my notes from the Baker trial. You had asked me earlier if one of the boys was a ringleader. So I found my transcripts from Dr. Hutchinson, the psychologist who testified during the trial. He told me off the record he was convinced Turner was the one responsible for the murder. He interviewed both kids and he said Turner led the charge. He said that Vance admitted purposefully missing when he threw rocks at Josh. Apparently Vance also had bruises from a beating he took from Turner."

"None of that was in the case file," I said.

"Because it never came out in court. Hutchinson testified to the boys' state of mind, but since they were tried together and since the boys never took the stand, no one ever asked him about who did what. It was just assumed that both kids went at it together."

"And you're sure he disagreed with that?"

"I'm positive," said Nell. "I have it right here in my notes. He said he'd stake his career on Turner being the alpha and Vance just following out of fear and intimidation. I found his contact information. He's retired but he might still talk to you if you want. That side of the story never came out, so if you're looking for a fresh angle this might be it."

"Thanks for the call, Nell, but I think I'm going to scrap the book. With Vance dead and Turner MIA I've got little to go on."

"Not even with the recent developments?"

"It makes for a good news story, but I can't sustain it for an entire book. Of course, you're welcome to run with it if you like."

"I'm enjoying retirement too much." She laughed. "I plan to follow the Thomas Vance case and file a few more pieces for the paper as a contributor, but doubt it'll go any further than that."

"What does special correspondent mean anyway?"

"It means they don't pay you." She laughed again. "Take care."

"You too."

I clicked off the phone and finished the last bit of coffee in my cup. I picked up the white envelope and rubbed it between my fingers.

I didn't know if Turner played me or not. I was convinced Vance ran the show back then and that Turner was just caught up in it all. Maybe Dr. Hutchinson was wrong, maybe not. I'd never know. I'd never know what happened that day thirty-two years ago, and I didn't want to. Sometimes it's better to forget, even if that means letting the voices fall silent and leaving the monsters far behind.

I stood up from the table, ripped the white envelope in half and dropped it into the stainless steel garbage can before walking outside.

As I walked toward my car, I approached a woman opening her station wagon's rear door. Two children bounded out and she quickly took hold of their wrists and checked for traffic. She offered me an awkward smile and I nodded back.

I wanted to believe I had levied some justice that went unserved so long ago, but the only thing I knew for certain was Josh's murder was proof that pure evil existed. It truly existed and it was capable of entering our safe little lives anytime it wanted and destroying us from the inside out. Maybe I didn't bring justice to Josh Baker, but it didn't mean I couldn't do it for someone else.

WILL FINN HARDING RETURN?

Will Finn Harding return? Maybe, but why not check out the Connor Harding series while the author makes up his mind? We suggest starting with:

Catch and Release

An ex-mob fixer must solve the murder of a hitman's wife and daughter before becoming the next victim.

Connor Harding is the go-to man when it comes to solving problems for the underworld's most dangerous criminals. Freddie Blasko is a violent hitman with a reputation for results. Twelve years after Freddie's wife and daughter were brutally killed, he wants Connor to solve their murders.

Freddie tracks Connor down at his secluded cabin in Maine, but Connor wants nothing to do with the job. He knows an unsolvable case when he sees one. Twelve years is a long time, and there's no evidence, no witnesses, and nothing to go on.

But, Freddie isn't the type to take no for an answer. He gives Connor an ultimatum: solve the case, or Connor's brother dies.

Fearing for his brother's life, Connor investigates the murders and slowly pieces the puzzle together. He uncovers a long-buried secret and quickly finds that no one, not even the victims, is who they seem.

What he doesn't know is that while he's tracking the killer, someone else is tracking him.

Can Connor find the murderer and save his brother before becoming the next victim?

GET A FREE NOVEL

Sign up for my newsletter to receive a free novel and exclusive updates at www.traceconger.com/freebies.

Please leave a review:
Like this book? Please consider leaving a review at your favorite online bookstore. Reviews from readers like you can help other readers find their next favorite read. And it's a great way to support your favorite authors.

ACKNOWLEDGMENTS

This novel would not have been possible without the generous support of several individuals. I'd like to thank the following people for their direct and indirect involvement in giving this project life:

Andrew Bockhold, Christine Grote, Scott High and Greg Petersen for reading and providing valuable feedback on early drafts; Elizabeth A. White for her editing expertise and taking these words to a higher level; Doug Hunter for being a sounding board and PI consultant; and Holly Hentz for her medical knowledge and continued friendship.

And a very special thank you to Beth Conger for her continued love, support and encouragement, and for letting me pretend to be a writer.

My sincere thanks to each of you.

ABOUT THE AUTHOR

Trace Conger is an award-winning author in the crime, thriller, and suspense genres. He writes the Connor Harding (Thriller) series and the Mr. Finn (PI) series, among others.

His Connor Harding series follows freelance "Mirage Man" Connor Harding as he solves problems for the world's most dangerous criminals. The Mr. Finn series follows private investigator Finn Harding as he straddles the fine line between right and wrong.

Conger won a Shamus Award for his debut novel, THE SHADOW BROKER. His suspense novella, THE WHITE BOY, won the Fresh Ink Award for Best Novella of 2020.

He is known for his tight writing style, dark themes, and subtle humor. Trace lives in Cincinnati with his wonderfully supportive family.

ALSO BY TRACE CONGER

Mr. Finn Series:

The Shadow Broker

Scar Tissue

The Prison Guard's Son

Connor Harding Series:

Catch and Release

Mirage Man

The Wicked Side

Standalones:

The White Boy

Five Will Die

www.ingramcontent.com/pod-product-compliance
Lightning Source LLC
Chambersburg PA
CBHW020722310726
48979CB00004B/1028

* 9 7 8 1 9 5 7 3 3 6 1 4 5 *